The angry words died on her lips at the sight of Jed standing beside the bed wearing nothing but a pair of faded denims.

In fact, she was having trouble breathing, let alone speaking!

Jed's chest and arms were as tanned as his face. His shoulders were wide and muscled, and a dark dusting of hair on his chest went down in a V to his stomach. There was not an ounce of superfluous flesh on his body.

Meg couldn't speak, couldn't move as she acknowledged that she should have knocked first—that of course Jed would be changing into the clothes her father had brought him.

Jed raised one dark brow at her continued silence. "I'm pretty sure I'm not the first half-naked man you've ever seen," he drawled.

MARRIAGE AND MISTLETOE

When millionaires claim Christmas brides...

Snow is falling, lights are sparkling, the scene is set—for winter seductions and festive white weddings!

Don't miss any of our exciting stories this month in Promotional Harlequin Presents! Available now, in December 2007:

The Rancher's Rules
Lucy Monroe

Her Husband's Christmas Bargain
Margaret Mayo

The Christmas Night Miracle
Carole Mortimer

The Italian Tycoon's Bride
Helen Brooks

THE CHRISTMAS NIGHT MIRACLE

CAROLE MORTIMER

MARRIAGE AND MISTLETOE

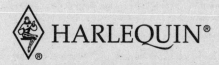

HARLEQUIN®

TORONTO • NEW YORK • LONDON
AMSTERDAM • PARIS • SYDNEY • HAMBURG
STOCKHOLM • ATHENS • TOKYO • MILAN • MADRID
PRAGUE • WARSAW • BUDAPEST • AUCKLAND

ISBN-13: 978-0-373-82059-7
ISBN-10:   0-373-82059-3

THE CHRISTMAS NIGHT MIRACLE

First North American Publication 2007.

Copyright © 2006 by Carole Mortimer.

www.eHarlequin.com

Printed in U.S.A.

CAROLE MORTIMER is one of Harlequin's most popular and prolific authors. Since her first novel, published in 1979, this British writer has shown no signs of slowing her pace. In fact, she has published more than 135 novels!

Her strong, traditional romances, with their distinct style, brilliantly developed characters and romantic plot twists, have earned her an enthusiastic audience worldwide.

Carole was born in a village in England that she claims was so small that "if you blinked as you drove through it you could miss seeing it completely!" She adds that her parents still live in the house where she first came into the world, and her two brothers live very close by.

Carole's early ambition to become a nurse came to an abrupt end after only one year of training due to a weakness in her back, suffered in the aftermath of a fall. Instead, she went on to work in the computer department of a well-known stationery company.

During her time there, Carole made her first attempt at writing a novel for Harlequin Books. "The manuscript was far too short and the plotline not up to standard, so I naturally received a rejection slip," she says. "Not taking rejection well, I went off in a sulk for two years before deciding to 'have another go.'" Her second manuscript was accepted, beginning a long and fruitful career. She says she has "enjoyed every moment of it!"

Carole lives "in a most beautiful part of Britain" with her husband and children.

"I really do enjoy my writing, and have every intention of continuing to do so for another twenty years!"

For Peter

CHAPTER ONE

'IT'S snowing again, Mummy!' Scott cried excitedly from the back of the car.

What an understatement.

It wasn't just snowing, it was blowing and gusting towards blizzard proportions. Which, in fact, the radio station Meg was listening to as she drove along had already warned that it would become some time this evening.

It had just been a flurry of delicate white snowflakes when they had left London three hours ago, pretty in its delicacy, to be admired and enjoyed, but standing no chance of actually settling on the streets of the busy city, even though some of it had clung determinedly to the rooftops.

Unfortunately, the further Meg had driven out of London, the heavier the snow had begun to fall, until it was now a thick layer on the ground, the road in front of her almost indistinguishable from the hedgerow, the snow hitting the windscreen so thickly the wipers were having a problem dealing with it.

As was Meg herself, finding it increasingly difficult to control the car as the wheels slipped and slid on the growing layer of snow, the fall of darkness just over an hour ago making things worse, the headlights just seeming to hit a wall of white rather than light the way.

Scott, at three and a half, and awake after sleeping in the back of the car for the last hour, could only see the potential fun and not the danger of this novelty in his young life.

Something Meg was at great pains to maintain as she glanced at him briefly in the rear-view mirror, her smile warm and loving as she looked at his tousled head of dark hair and still-sleepy features; one of them feeling worried and panicked was quite enough.

'Isn't it lovely?' she agreed as she hastily returned her attention to the road, the car having slewed slightly sideways in that moment of distraction.

She shouldn't have come by car. The train would have been so much easier. And at least if there had been a problem with snow on the rails she would have had adult company in her misery.

Because she hadn't seen another car, or even a truck, in the last half an hour.

Of course, that could have something to do with the warning being given out on the radio station for the last hour by the police for people 'not to travel unless absolutely necessary'. A warning that had come far too late for Meg, already more than two thirds of the way towards her destination.

'Can I build a snowman when we get to Granma and Grandad's?' Scott prompted hopefully, thankfully still totally unaware of their precarious situation.

'Of course, darling,' she agreed distractedly.

The relevant word in Scott's statement was 'when'—because Meg was very much afraid they weren't going to make it to her parents' house this evening, as planned.

She could barely see where she was going now, the headlights of the car only seeming to make the snow whiter and brighter, and blinding. If she could just see a house, or even a public house, anything that showed signs of habitation, then she could stop and ask them for help.

'I need the toilet, Mummy.'

Her hands tightened instinctively on the steering wheel; this was, Meg had quickly learnt after toilet-training her young son two years ago, the age-old cry guaranteed to put any mother into a panic. Because it always came when you were standing in a long queue at the supermarket, or sitting on a bus, or trying on shoes—or in the middle of a blinding snowstorm.

And something else she had also learnt very quickly: it was no good telling a small child that they would have to wait a few minutes while you finished what you were doing—when children said they needed the toilet, then they needed it now.

Nevertheless, like many other mothers before her, Meg tried. 'Can you hang on a few minutes, Scott? We aren't too far from Granma and Grandad's now,' she added with more hope than actual knowledge; she had absolutely no idea where they were, as she hadn't been able to see a signpost for miles.

'I need the toilet now, Mummy,' Scott came back predictably.

She was already so tense from concentrating on her driving that her shoulders and arms ached, this added pressure only making the tension worse. Not that it was Scott's fault. He had been asleep for over an hour; of course he needed the toilet.

But she could hardly pull over to the side of the road, even if she could find it, take Scott outside and just let him go to the loo there. This wasn't the middle of summer, it was the evening before Christmas Eve, with a temperature below zero. She could hardly expect him to expose himself to the elements.

If only she could find somewhere, a building of some kind, a barn, even, so very appropriate for this time of year, somewhere they could go and sit this thing out.

Even as the thought played across her frantic mind she felt the steering go from her completely, the car moving sideways as it slid across the snow.

'Hang on, Scott,' Meg had time to warn before she saw a dark shape looming towards her in the darkness, the car coming to a shuddering halt as it hit an immovable object, the noise of the impact almost deafening in the otherwise eerie silence created by the blanket of snow.

'Mummy? Mummy!' Scott's voice rose hysterically at her lack of response.

'It's all right, Scott,' she soothed reassuringly even as she put up a hand to where seconds ago her head had made painful contact with the window beside her.

Amazingly, although the engine had stalled on impact, the headlights were still on, and when Meg turned she could see Scott strapped into his seat in the back of the car, tears streaming down his cheeks as he tried to reach forward and touch her.

'It's all right, baby.' She choked back her own tears

as she saw and felt his fear, fumbling with the clasp of her seat belt, desperate to get out of the car and go to him, to hold him, to reassure him they were both okay.

But before she could do any of that the door beside her was wrenched open, letting in a blast of icy-cold air, Meg's face white with shock as she let out a scream at the apparition she saw looming there.

'Mummy, it's a bear!' Scott cried from the back of the car.

A big hairy grizzly bear.

A blue-eyed grizzly bear, Meg realized as the man pushed back the hood of the heavy coat he was wearing, snow instantly falling on the dark thickness of his hair.

'Are you okay?' he barked concernedly, the narrowed blue gaze turning to Scott as he began to cry in the back of the car.

'I have to go to him!' Meg muttered anxiously as she scrambled out of the car, the man stepping back as she pushed past him to wrench open the back door and almost fling herself inside. 'It's okay, Scott. We're okay.' She held him close to her, feeling his shuddering tears. 'This nice man has only come to help us.' She hoped.

It would be just her luck to have crashed into the side of the house—yes, she could see it now, the lights burning warmly inside, she had actually hit the side of a house!—of an eccentric recluse who didn't like women and children, and had no intention of helping them, either.

Although at this particular moment she didn't really care who or what the man was; she was too weary, too upset, to do more than look up at him with huge shadowed green eyes and say, 'Is there any room at the inn?'

Which was a totally ridiculous thing for her to have said, she realized, still cringing inwardly a few minutes later when she and Scott, after a quick visit to the loo for her small son, sat together in front of a warm, crackling log fire drinking hot chocolate.

Although their rescuer had simply looked at her with mocking blue eyes and replied, 'Sorry to break with tradition, but, yes, there's room at the inn,' before all but picking her and Scott up in his arms—no little weight, she was sure—and carrying them inside the house.

Well, it wasn't exactly a house, Meg noted as she took a look around her, more of a cottage with its low beamed ceilings and small rooms. Not that it mattered what it was; it was warm, and dry, and out of the snowstorm still raging outside.

A storm their unexpected host had gone back out into after making them the hot chocolate.

Scott, safely ensconced on her denim-clad knees, peered shyly around her shoulder towards the door. 'Where did the man go, Mummy?'

Good question. But apart from 'outside', she had no idea.

'The name's Jed,' the man drawled as he stepped back into the small sitting-room, looking more like a bear than ever, the heavy coat and hood liberally covered in the same snow that dripped off in lumps from the huge boots he wore. 'Yours.' He handed Meg the handbag that she had left on the passenger seat of the car. 'And yours,' he added more gently as he gave Scott a small knapsack that contained the toys he had brought along to play with on the journey. 'Your car keys.' He dropped them into Meg's waiting palm. 'Not that I think anyone is going to steal your car any time soon,' he added dryly as he shrugged out of the heavy coat. 'You dinged the front pretty bad.'

Two things had become obvious during that conversation, or should that be monologue? Because Meg's teeth were still chattering too badly for her to be able to answer him. One, that the man's accent was American, two, that he didn't look much less formidable without the bulky coat.

At well over six feet in height, with shaggy dark hair; his shoulders were wide beneath the black sweater, faded denims fitting snugly on narrow hips and powerful thighs, those deep blue eyes set in a face of teaked mahogany, the squareness of his jaw giving him an air of complete self-assurance.

Meg's arms tightened instinctively about Scott as that vivid blue gaze moved over the two of them with the same deliberation, knowing what he would see: a woman of five feet two inches tall, with a mane of straight dark hair that reached almost to her waist, a small, heart-shaped face, green eyes, with a sprinkling of freckles across her nose, the little boy on her knee with the same colouring and freckles.

And the silence in the room, apart from the crackling of the logs on the fire, was starting to become oppressive.

Meg stirred herself. 'I'm really sorry to have disturbed you and your family in this way, Mr—er, Jed,' she amended awkwardly.

'No family, just me,' he dismissed easily, moving into a crouched position to place another log on the fire.

'Hey,' he murmured steadyingly as Meg and Scott moved further to the back of the chair. 'I realize I haven't been near a barber for a couple of months, but I don't really look like a bear, do I?' He gave what Meg was sure was meant to be a reassuring smile, but only succeeded in making him look more wolfish rather than harmless.

Meg moistened dry lips. The storm and crash must have made her oversensitive; this man was their rescuer, not their attacker. 'I really can't thank you enough for helping us like this, Mr—Jed,' she said again ruefully, placing Scott back on the chair as she stood up. 'Without your help Scott and I may just have…well, I can't thank you enough.' She decided not to go into the details of what could have befallen Scott and herself out there alone in the storm. Scott was probably going to have nightmares about this as it was, without making things worse.

'You're welcome,' he drawled dryly as he stood up to tower over her once again.

Meg blinked up at him. He really was extremely large for this tiny room. 'If you could provide me with the telephone number of a local garage, I'll give them a call and see if they can perhaps tow my car away before taking us to the nearest… No?' she said uncertainly as the man gave a derisive shake of his head.

'No,' he confirmed. 'It's after five-thirty, so the workshop at the garage in town will be closed. And even if it wasn't I doubt very much they would come out in this weather. Don't you?' He glanced pointedly out of the cottage window where the snow was still falling heavily.

She glanced at Scott who, having lost interest in this

adult conversation, was now taking toys out of his bag to play with. Which was probably just as well—there was absolutely no need for him to see his mother's worry.

What was she going to do? The car, from what this man said, was undriveable. The snow was still falling, and even the few minutes she had spent outside between the car and cottage were enough to tell her she couldn't expect Scott to walk anywhere in that.

Besides which, she had absolutely no idea where she was.

Jed watched as the emotions flickered across the woman's face, although 'woman' was perhaps stretching things a bit. Despite the small boy who called her 'Mummy', she didn't look much more than a child herself, barely five feet tall, her face appearing bare of make-up, her only colour the freckles across her nose and the emerald-green eyes surrounded by the longest black lashes he had ever seen, her long, glowing black hair unstyled except for a few wisps on her forehead.

And she appeared to be quietly panicking from her pained expression and continuing pallor.

Not that he was all that happy with this turn of events himself. He hadn't deliberately placed himself out of circulation here in the middle of nowhere to have his peace and solitude shattered by a green-eyed imp and her kid.

But whatever panic she was still feeling over her predicament was placed firmly under control as she introduced herself. 'I'm Meg Hamilton—' she even managed a slight curve of those full lips as she held out a slender hand '—and this is my son, Scott,' she added with a certain amount of pride as she gazed down at the little kid now busily playing with a tractor and some farm animals.

Trust the English, Jed mused ruefully. Even in the middle of a blizzard, good manners couldn't be ignored.

'Jed Cole,' he returned abruptly, searching her face for any sign of recognition of his name as he shook her hand.

'Mr Cole.' But she only seemed relieved to have the formalities covered, as though these minor pleasantries re-assured her, at the same time releasing her hand from his.

She didn't recognize either his name or him, then. That, or else she was a very good actress, followed the cynical thought.

Over the last nine months, since his life had suddenly become public property, women had tried all sorts of tricks to meet him, one of them even sneaking into the sports club he belonged to and accosting him in the shower. Apparently all the other men present in the changing-room had been too dazed by the woman being there at all to ask her what she thought she was doing.

Although perhaps dragging a kid along, in the middle of a snowstorm, was going a little far, even for the most ardent fan. And from the totally unknowing look on Meg Hamilton's face, she wasn't one of those.

'Is there perhaps a hotel nearby?' Meg queried with what he thought was more hope than expectation.

'I hate to disappoint you, Mrs Hamilton.' And he really did, already resenting this intrusion into his privacy.

Not that he would have just left her and the kid outside to freeze—he just wished she had chosen someone else's cottage to drive in to.

But having been secluded here for two months

now—not very productive months, he had to admit—
he had got out of the habit of polite conversation. If he
had ever had it. Which he probably hadn't, he acknowledged ruefully. He didn't suffer fools gladly at the best
of times, and driving in this weather, with a little kid in
tow, had to be the height of foolishness.

'No hotel,' he rasped. 'In fact, apart from this cottage,
no anything,' he bit out harshly.

A frown marred that creamy brow now. 'But we can't
be too far from Winston. Can we…?' she added uncertainly, those small, slender hands betraying her nervousness as she ran them against denim-clad thighs.

She should be nervous, risking her own life and that
of the kid's, to drive in weather like this, and for what?
He had no idea, but it wasn't worth it, whatever the reason.

His impatient anger was audible in his tone. 'About
ten miles or so, though it might as well be a hundred,'
he added harshly as her expression brightened. 'You
must have taken a wrong turning half a mile or so away,
because this is a private road that leads to this cottage
only. And even if they get the snowploughs out tomorrow
the road to the cottage will remain snowbound.'

Tell it like it is, why don't you, Cole? he berated
himself disgustedly as tears swam now in those deep
green eyes.

But if she hadn't deliberately come here to meet
him—and he was inclined to believe that she hadn't, her
distress was too genuine—then what was this wom-
an/child doing out here in the middle of nowhere two
days before Christmas?

He scowled heavily. 'Where have you driven from?'

'London,' she said flatly. 'It wasn't snowing when we set out—well, not much, anyway,' she amended with a grimace as her son would have spoken.

Out of the mouths of babes. But Jed accepted that it probably hadn't been snowing anything like this in the capital; he had never known snow to settle for long during his own frequent trips to that busy metropolis. But London was over a hundred and twenty miles away from here, at least.

'Didn't you have the good sense to pull over and stop somewhere when you could see the weather was worsening?' he snapped his impatience with the situation, what was he supposed to do with this unlikely pair of visitors?

'Obviously not!' A flush brightened her cheeks. 'I realize now that I should have done,' she continued awkwardly, those green eyes glittering with anger now rather than tears. 'But I didn't.' She angled her pointed chin challengingly, as if daring him to criticize her again.

It was a challenge Jed had no problem accepting. 'Instead of which, you and the kid there are now my guests!' Unwelcome guests, he could have added, but knew that his tone of voice said it all.

Her mouth set stubbornly. 'The kid's name is Scott,' she corrected tersely, obviously smarting from his comments. 'And I'm sure there must be some way the two of us can get out of here and leave you to your privacy.' The last word came out scornfully.

That privacy wasn't something to be scorned as far as he was concerned; it had been hard won.

But it was hard not to admire this petite woman. Not

only had she kept her head through blizzard conditions—simply pulling over to the side of the road and sitting out the storm could have resulted in her and her son freezing to death—and maintained that calm after the crash, but she still had enough courage left to stand up to her reluctant rescuer.

And he was reluctant, had no idea what he was going to do with the pair of them for what he knew, even if Meg Hamilton hadn't realized it yet, was going to be an overnight stay, at least.

Jed Cole to the rescue. It wasn't a role he, or indeed many of his friends, would ever have imagined him in. Humanity, he had decided this last year—even ebony-haired green-eyed waifs—left a lot to be desired, and should be avoided, if possible.

Something, in this particular situation, he simply couldn't do. Which only increased his bad temper.

'Really?' He dropped down into the unoccupied armchair, draping a leg over the arm as he looked up at her enquiringly. 'I would be very interested to hear it?' He quirked dark brows.

'Maybe we could walk to—'

'There's a blizzard raging outside,' Jed cut in impatiently. 'Some of the drifts are already four feet high; if the kid—Scott,' he amended dryly as she glared at him. 'If he fell into one of those drifts you'd never find him.'

Once again he watched as the emotions raging inside her showed on her face; good manners versus impatient anger this time, rather than her earlier panic at her predicament.

Anger won out as she glared at him. 'I would find him,' she assured him grimly.

He would just bet that she would too, reminding him at that moment of a lioness protecting her cub.

He shrugged. 'You got lost driving a car; what chance do you think you stand on foot?'

That glare turned to a frown as she moved to stand protectively in front of her son before answering him softly. 'Are you deliberately trying to frighten me?'

Jed eyed her speculatively. 'Am I succeeding?' he prompted dryly.

'You're being unnecessarily cruel, if that's what you mean,' she came back tartly.

Giving a good impression of one of the bantam hens back home on his parents' farm as she defended her ground against one of the larger species of live-stock. A defence that was usually successful, he recalled wryly.

'Look, I realize we've inconvenienced you, turning up like this...'

'You drove into the side of the damned cottage,' he reminded with some of the incredulity he had felt at the time. Relaxing beside the log fire, staring broodingly into the flickering flames as he sipped a glass of whisky, he had heard an almighty bang as the whole cottage had seemed to shudder. He had thought the side of the cottage was going to fall in on him.

'Well. Yes... I know, but—' she gave a pained grimace '—I didn't mean to,' she added ruefully. 'And could you please not swear in front of Scott?' she said softly. 'They aren't words I want added to his vocabulary.'

Not only had he been severely 'inconvenienced', he was now being told what he could or couldn't say.

He scowled darkly. 'Is there a Mr Hamilton somewhere anxiously awaiting your arrival?' If there was, he would quite happily pass on the responsibility of rescuing his wife and son to the other man.

She looked stunned for a moment, as if reminded of something she had forgotten as the angry flush faded from her cheeks, making her look all eyes again. Defenceless eyes, Jed recognized uncomfortably.

She chewed on her bottom lip before answering him. 'Yes, there's a Mr Hamilton.'

'Nearby, I hope?' Jed prompted harshly, not happy with the protective emotion this woman was starting to engender in him. If he could just get her back to her life he could return to his.

'And a Mrs Hamilton,' she continued distractedly. 'My parents,' she supplied at his quizzical frown.

Her parents, Mr and Mrs Hamilton. Which meant there wouldn't be a husband rushing to the rescue, because there wasn't a husband.

'I was on my way to see them for Christmas when I—' her bottom lip trembled slightly before she drew in a deeply controlling breath and continued '—before I got lost. Do you think I might use your telephone to call them?' That pointed chin was once again raised challengingly. 'My father hasn't been well, and they would have expected us to have arrived by now.'

Jed frowned. Not 'they will be worried about me and their grandson', just they would have 'expected us to have arrived by now'.

He shook the observation off impatiently; he was probably just reading too much into it. What the hell business of his was it, anyway?

'Sure.' He made a sweeping gesture to where the telephone sat on the table by the door.

The old-fashioned kind of telephone before push buttons. But, then, everything about this cottage was a bit dated, he had discovered when he'd arrived here nine weeks ago. From the sheets and blankets on the beds rather than duvets, to the fire. And he had lost count of the amount of times he had cracked his head on one low-beamed ceiling or another during the first couple of weeks here, before he'd learnt to duck automatically as he stood up.

Not that Meg Hamilton had that problem, he noted a little sourly as she moved to pick up the receiver, her ebony head at least a foot lower than those innocuous-looking, but actually lethal, beams.

No, her nervousness seemed to be for another reason entirely.

He stood up. 'Would you like me to take Scott into the kitchen and give you some privacy for your call?' He had no idea what made him make the offer, only that he sensed her reluctance to make the call.

She gave him a startled look before glancing past him to where her son was still playing with his tractor. 'No, I... That's okay. Thank you.' She gave a brief smile. 'I only need to let them know I won't be arriving in time for dinner, after all.' She picked up the receiver and dialled.

Jed made no answer as he lowered his considerable height back into the armchair. But he thought about what that told him. For instance, if his mother had been expecting him to arrive in the middle of a snowstorm, and he hadn't done so, she would have called out the local police, probably the FBI, plus sent his father and two brothers out to search for him. A bit over the top, maybe, but in those circumstances dinner would be the last thing on his mother's mind.

'Mother?' Meg Hamilton queried tautly as her call was answered. 'Yes, I'm sorry. It will probably be some time tomorrow now. Yes, I realize that. Of course I'll let you know if we intend arriving in time for lunch.' There was a slight pause as she listened to a lengthy reply. 'Did she?' Meg's voice had become somewhat brittle now. 'Yes, I probably should have come by train, too, but I had Scott's things to bring too, and… Yes, I'll definitely call you tomorrow to confirm our arrival.' Her hand, Jed noticed frowningly, was shaking slightly as she replaced the receiver.

It sounded as if his instincts had been correct. Mrs Hamilton, at least, was more concerned with her dining arrangements than she was with the welfare of her daughter and grandson.

He glanced at Scott as he sat in front of the fire arranging his farm animals on the rug. As far as Jed was aware his grandmother hadn't said one word about him.

Jed straightened in the chair as he recognized what he was doing. He would not get involved. This girl and her son would be on their way as soon as he could get them there, and that would be the end of them as far as he was concerned.

He would not get involved.

CHAPTER TWO

MEG deliberately kept her back to the room for several seconds after the call had ended, taking the time to try and compose herself.

Her palms were damp and yet she felt an icy shiver down her spine—not an unusual reaction after talking to her mother.

She had no idea how her mother did it; perhaps the tone of voice her mother used rather than the actual words spoken, she thought. All Meg knew was that after a five-minute conversation with her mother she felt five years old again, rather than a grown woman with a young son of her own.

But that wasn't all of it, of course. Her sister Sonia would be there for Christmas, indeed, as her mother had just told her, was already there, having sensibly taken the train, her skiing trip cancelled because her husband had sprained his ankle on the golf course and so couldn't ski.

Sonia, of the designer clothes, the successful career, and the eminently suitable marriage.

Everything, as their mother was so fond of reminding, that Meg wasn't, and didn't have.

She bought her clothes from a chain store, and her career as an interior designer kept the landlord from the door and the bills paid, with very little left over for anything else. As for marriage, she had Scott instead of the suitable husband her mother would have preferred.

And he was better than any husband she might have had, worth all the heartache of the last three and a half years, she reflected with the same fierce protectiveness she had known from the first moment he had been placed in her arms.

Sonia could keep her wealthy lifestyle, and her suitable marriage; Meg would much rather have Scott.

'I was just about to fix supper when you arrived.' Jed Cole spoke huskily behind her.

Meg drew herself up, turning to face him, putting all thoughts of Sonia and her parents to the back of her mind. There would be plenty of time for her to think of them tomorrow. Or even the day after that, she acknowledged ruefully after a glance outside at the still heavily falling snow.

Right now she had the more immediate problem of being a guest in Jed Cole's cottage—an unwelcome guest, if her guess was correct.

And who could blame him for feeling that way? She hadn't exactly arrived under auspicious circumstances. Crashing into the side of the cottage like that. The poor man must have wondered what on earth was going on.

Where the splutter of laughter came from she wasn't exactly sure, only that it was there, and there wasn't a thing she could do about it. In fact, the more she tried to control it, the worse it became.

'I'm sorry.' She shook her head helplessly. 'I just—I can't believe I actually drove into the side of your cottage.' She was laughing so hard now there were tears on her cheeks.

'Why's Mummy crying?' Scott looked across at her concernedly.

'I have no idea,' Jed Cole answered him grimly even as he took a determined step towards her. 'Will you calm it down?' he snapped. 'You're scaring the kid.'

As Scott didn't look scared, only puzzled by her behaviour, it was more likely she was scaring 'the man' rather than 'the kid', Jed Cole staring down at her uncertainly now, as if he weren't sure whether to shake her or slap her.

Neither of which particularly appealed to her, although she had a feeling he might enjoy it.

'I really am sorry.' She did her best to stop laughing, wiping the tears from her cheeks as she met his gaze. 'You were about to make supper, you said?' The hysteria hadn't completely gone, was still lurking on the edges, but for the moment she seemed to have it under control.

Jed Cole still eyed her warily, those hard hewn features appearing more arrogant than ever, his jaw clenched disapprovingly. 'Steak and fries,' he answered her abruptly. 'There's enough for two if you're interested,' he added tersely. 'Although quite what you're going to feed the kid—'

'His name is Scott,' she repeated firmly. 'And Scott eats what I eat.'

The man grimaced. 'Then I guess there's enough steak and fries for three.' He turned on his heel and left the room abruptly, the sound of another door opening and then closing seconds later.

Meg gave Scott a quick glance. He seemed satisfied that his mother was okay after all and had resumed playing with his toys. 'Scott, I'm going to help Mr Cole prepare dinner. Do you want to come or stay here and play?' There was a guard in front of the fire, and he was playing far enough away not to come to any harm.

'I stay here,' he decided predictably. 'There's no tree, Mummy,' he added with a frown.

No tree. No decorations. No cards. In fact, nothing to indicate it was Christmas Eve tomorrow.

'Not everyone celebrates Christmas in the way we do, Scott,' she explained smilingly. 'And I'm sure Granma and Grandad will have a big tree for you to look at tomorrow.'

The tree would be in the hallway as always, with the decorations all just so, and white lights only because her mother abhorred the coloured ones, with neatly rib-boned and bowed gifts nestled beneath it.

A sharp contrast to the fern they had left behind in their flat, Meg thought wistfully, with its home-made decorations and paper chains, and enough tinsel and multicoloured lights draped around it to illuminate a tree four times its size.

'I'm just in the kitchen helping Mr Cole, darling.' She bent to kiss her son lightly on top of his ebony head. 'Just call if you need me.'

It wasn't too difficult to locate the kitchen in this three-up three-down cottage. The door to the room opposite the sitting-room was open, revealing a small formal dining-room, meaning the closed door at the end of the hallway had to be the kitchen.

But even without that process of elimination, the sound of pots banging and the smell of food cooking would have told her exactly where she could find Jed Cole.

Jed Cole.

He really was something of an enigma. Even without that American accent he so obviously didn't belong here. He was too big, or else the cottage was too small for him. Besides, the décor and furniture in the cottage were both well-worn and faded, and even if she didn't buy expensive clothing herself Meg knew a cashmere sweater when she saw one, and the faded denims had an expensive label on the back pocket, the shoes he had put on after taking off the heavy boots made from soft black leather.

'So tell me,' she said brightly as she entered the kitchen to find him putting steaks, two of them, under the grill. 'Which do you think you would have opted for if I hadn't stopped laughing when I did—the shaking or the slap?'

Jed eyed her mockingly from beneath heavy dark brows as he leant back against one of the kitchen units, arms folded across the width of his chest as he looked down at her. 'Actually, I'd got around to thinking that kissing you might do the trick,' he drawled ruefully.

Embarrassed colour instantly stained her cheeks. So much for her attempt at humour.

'But on second thoughts,' he added hardly, 'I decided that I'm not into kissing teenage mothers, no matter what the provocation!'

Meg's eyes widened at this description of her. 'Just how old do you think I am?'

He gave her a considering look. 'Obviously old enough to legally be the mother of the—Scott,' he amended harshly. 'Just, probably.'

She put her hands on her hips as she eyed him incredulously. 'For your information, Mr Cole, I'm twenty-seven years old,' she snapped. 'And I most certainly did not offer you any provocation.' The wings of colour in her cheeks seemed to burn now.

His eyes narrowed at the slight emphasis she put on the 'you', that steely blue gaze easily holding hers for several long seconds, until finally he gave a shrug and moved away. 'Make the salad, why don't you?' he instructed tersely before checking the steaks under the grill. 'Nothing ever looks as bad with a hot meal inside you.'

'Does that apply to you or to me?' Meg returned ruefully as she moved to take the makings of a salad out of the cooler box in the fridge.

'Both of us!' he came back tersely before turning away to look at the fries.

Meg continued to look at him for several seconds. This really wasn't an ideal situation, for any of them. Jed Cole had just been sitting here in the cottage minding his own business, looking forward to his steak dinner no doubt, and now he had a woman and her young son to feed too.

She moved to look out of the kitchen window, the light reflected outside showing her that the gusting wind was blowing the snow into deep drifts.

'Is there really no way we can get away from here tonight?'

She only realized she had spoken the words out loud

when Jed Cole slammed a knife down on the worktop. 'No way and no how,' he rasped with controlled violence. 'Now if you want to eat tonight, I suggest you make the damn salad.'

Meg had turned as he'd slammed down the utensil, eyeing him warily now as she started to prepare the salad.

'And stop looking at me like that,' he added impatiently.

She straightened. 'Like what?'

'Like a mouse expecting to be mauled by that bear Scott originally thought that I was!' He sighed his exasperation. 'Compared to my usual demeanour I'm behaving like a goddamned pussycat, okay?'

Meg bit on her top lip as it twitched with laughter. At the moment he looked as Scott used to when he'd gone through 'the terrible twos', totally disgruntled at not being able to get his own way.

'Okay,' she agreed mildly. 'Do you want dressing on this salad?'

'Do I want…' He closed his eyes, drawing in a controlling breath before opening them again to glare at her. 'Who the hell are you, Meg Hamilton? And what warped quirk of fate,' he rasped before she could reply, 'landed you on my doorstep?'

'Actually it was the side of the cottage,' she corrected softly as she mixed a mustard dressing together. 'But we won't argue the details just now,' she dismissed brightly.

'We'll save that until later, huh?' he muttered, a grudging respect now in those deep blue eyes as he looked at her consideringly. 'What was with your mother earlier? She seemed more concerned with her eating arrangements than whether or not you and Scott were okay.'

The kitchen, small at best, with barely enough room for the two of them to move around it, suddenly didn't even seem big enough for that, with no room for her to hide, to avoid the piercing intrusion of Jed Cole's gaze.

Because he was right. Not once during that brief conversation had her mother bothered to ask why Meg and Scott had been delayed, merely commenting that her sister had managed to get there, also from London, because she had sensibly come by train.

It simply hadn't been worth the effort of explaining that, unlike Sonia, who had probably got all her Christmas presents for the family in one elegant designer-label bag after being gift-wrapped by the store they were bought from, Meg had all Scott's Father Christmas presents to bring too. Gifts lovingly bought and wrapped by Meg herself, this being the first Christmas that Scott, aged three and a half, had really appreciated and looked forward to. She had even gone to the expense of hiring a car so that she could transport the things here.

The car that was now crumpled into the side of the cottage.

She would have to call the hire company in the morning and explain what had happened, sincerely hoping that the insurance would cover the costs of the damage.

She managed to give Jed Cole a casual shrug as he stood waiting for an answer to his questions. 'Mothers are like that,' she evaded. 'Feeding their family is of high priority.'

Which might have been true of her mother if she did the cooking herself, but ever since Meg had been born, probably before that too, Mrs Sykes—Bessie—had presided over the Hamilton kitchen. But as Jed Cole would never meet her mother, let alone eat a meal in the Hamilton household, he didn't need to know that.

'I'm sure your mother is the same,' she dismissed.

There was a slight softening of his expression. 'For as long as I can remember my mother has always had enough extra food in the house to feed a family of ten, and often has, and if she hadn't she'd send my dad out to kill a cow.'

'She sounds nice,' Meg murmured wistfully, almost able to imagine the warm kitchen and the motherly figure there caring for her family.

'She is.' Jed nodded. 'So's my dad. And my two younger brothers. And their wives, and the numerous offspring they've produced.'

Meg gave him a considering look. 'So why aren't you there for Christmas, instead of—well, here, alone?'

His mouth twisted. 'Maybe because I prefer "alone" to my Mum and Dad, two younger brothers, their wives, and numerous offspring.'

Maybe.

And then again, maybe not.

She certainly hadn't imagined that softening when he'd spoken of his family, or the slightly wistful tone in his voice.

But she didn't have time to probe any further before he snapped, 'Will you stop asking so many questions, woman, and dish the food up?'

In other words, end of discussion about his family.

But that didn't stop Meg's curiosity about them, about

whether or not Mum, Dad, two brothers, their wives and their numerous offspring were sad because one of their number was missing from their Christmas this year.

Somehow, and she didn't know why she felt that way, she had a feeling that they were.

Mistake, Cole, Jed remonstrated with himself even while he inwardly acknowledged that the dressing on the salad was just as he liked it. But he should never have mentioned the idea of kissing Meg. Because now he couldn't take his eyes off her mouth. It was a rather nice mouth, too, the lips full, with a permanent tilt at their corners, as if this woman liked to smile a lot.

As she was smiling now at her small son as they all sat at the dining table and Scott manfully tried to tackle his own small piece of steak, fries and salad.

And she most definitely was a woman, and not a girl, he accepted self-derisively, her smart comeback before dinner that of an adult. And the soft swell beneath the dark green sweater she wore over faded denims was adult too, as was the curve of her hips. And as for those full, inviting lips.

Damn it, he should never have mentioned kissing her, because now he couldn't think of anything else!

Two months he had been holed up here, that was all, and now he was looking at Meg Hamilton as if she were a bottle of water in the desert. A carton of ice cream in a heatwave.

'Is the food not to your liking?'

Jed focused on her scowlingly. 'What?'

She gave him a quizzical smile. 'You were glaring at

your steak as if it had done something to offend you,'
she teased.

Oh, very funny. Ha, bloody ha.

It was okay for her to laugh, she wasn't the one sitting
here having carnal thoughts about a woman who had
arrived on his doorstep in distress, her young fatherless
son in tow.

'The food's fine,' he rasped curtly. 'It's all fine.' As
if to prove his point he stabbed a piece of steak on his
fork and shoved it into his mouth and began chewing.

And chewing.

Maybe cutting the steak down a little in size might
have been a good idea, Jed, he berated himself, aware
that both Meg and her son were now looking at him, Meg
surreptitiously Scott with the frank intensity of a child.

'It's rude to stare, Scott,' his mother remonstrated as
she noticed his intensity of concentration.

The little boy turned away obediently. Only to turn
back again seconds later when his mother wasn't
looking, those green eyes studied on Jed's face.

Obviously he had never seen a man try to eat half a
cow in one mouthful before.

'Mr Cole, why don't you have a tree?' Scott finally
asked, a frown marring his creamy brow.

Ah, it wasn't the steak that was bothering him at all.

'Or decorations?' The little boy looked disapproving
now. 'We like decorations, don't we, Mummy? An'
there's no cards, either,' Scott continued before his mother
could answer him. 'With robins on. We like robins, don't
we, Mummy?' He gave his mother a beatific smile.

As little kids went, this one was a cute little devil, Jed

allowed as he finally managed to swallow the steak. In fact, with his dark hair, green eyes, the freckles on his little nose, he was a tiny version of his mother.

Not again.

Meg Hamilton, even without the extra baggage, was most definitely not his type.

At thirty-eight, he liked his women to be tall and so-phisticated, older women, who were only interested in the brief relationship he was willing to give. Meg had the look of a woman who had already taken enough blows to her girlhood dreams, without another selfish bastard coming along to shatter them some more.

'I did explain, Scott—' Meg spoke quietly to her son now '—that not everyone celebrates Christmas.'

'Do you celebrate Christmas, Mr Cole?' Scott questioned guilelessly.

'Well… Yes. Usually.' Talk about putting him on the spot. 'But, you see, I don't actually live here, Scott. I live in a place called New York.' He predicted what the next question would be and answered it. 'Very far away from here, in a place called America.' Where, no doubt, dozens of cards and gifts would be waiting for him to deal with when he returned.

But even in New York he wouldn't have put up a tree and decorations, had never seen the need for them when there was only him living there, the modern chrome and leather of his apartment not lending themselves to such frivolity.

Scott's eyes were wide now, surrounded by the same incredibly long lashes as those of his mother. 'Then why are you here and not there?'

Exactly like his mother, Jed identified impatiently, who had asked him a similar question before dinner.

But the difference here was that with cute little kids like Scott you didn't feel comfortable either fobbing them off or lying to them.

However, at this point in time, Jed really didn't feel like telling the little boy the truth, either. Especially as there hadn't been so much as a flicker of recognition in Meg's face when he'd introduced himself earlier.

He wasn't quite sure where Meg had been for the last nine months while the invasion of his privacy had become a thing of nightmares, so that he had come to England and hidden away in this cottage in order to find the peace and quiet he needed to work. Not that he had worked. Well…not much, anyway. But this escape from instant recognition was better than nothing.

'I think we've bothered Mr Cole enough for one evening, Scott.' Meg came smoothly to his rescue at his continued silence. 'It's almost time for your bath and then bed.'

'Oh, but, Mummy, Father Christmas comes tomorrow night,' the little boy protested.

She smiled. 'All the more reason for you to get lots of sleep tonight. Let's help Mr Cole clear away, and then I'll run your bath—' She broke off, giving Jed a wry look. 'I take there is hot water for a bath?'

He nodded. 'And a shower, of sorts.' He stood up. 'You'll need your bags from the car?' He didn't particularly relish the idea of going back out into the cold and wet, but neither did he think it a good idea for Meg to be wandering about naked upstairs later. It might be fun,

but after the thoughts he had been having about the cur-
viness of her hips, and the soft warmth of her body, it
probably wasn't the best idea.

In fact, having this unlikely pair here at all wasn't a
particularly good idea, but as none of them had any
choice in the matter he would have to make the best of
it. And that included providing Meg with nightclothes.

'Please.' She nodded. 'Just the one bag in the boot
of the car.'

'Travelling light?' He raised dark brows, remembering all the clutter his sisters-in-law always seemed to
carry around for their kids.

'We're only staying at my parents' until Boxing Day,'
Meg answered him as she collected the plates together,
at the same time, it seemed, carefully avoiding his gaze.

They didn't have Boxing Day in the States, made do
with Christmas Eve and Christmas Day for the holidays
over there, but it seemed to him that Meg had travelled
a long way for a three-day, now two-day, visit. Why?

'We're going to see my granma and grandad,' Scot
told him brightly.

'So I understand.' Jed nodded, finding himself
smiling at the little boy in spite of himself.

Children, especially little ones like this, were not
part of his everyday life. Although, despite what he
might have said earlier, he was fond enough of his
nieces and nephews.

'Do you know my granma and grandad?' Scot looked
up at him expectantly.

He gave a shake of his head. 'I can't say that I've ever
met them, no.'

'Scott, it really is time for your—'

'Neither have I.' Scott spoke at the same time as his mother, his expression wistful now.

Curiouser and curiouser, Jed mulled frowningly. Scott had to be at least three, perhaps a little older, and yet he claimed never to have met his own grandparents. Jed could understand the lapse where the boy's father's parents were concerned, but not with his maternal grandparents.

What sort of people were the Hamiltons never to have even met their own grandson?

CHAPTER THREE

'Is it all right if I come in?' Meg hesitated in the doorway to the sitting room.

She had just put Scott up to bed in the guest bedroom—a guest bedroom with a double bed that she and Scott could share, thank goodness. Scott was a restless sleeper, and she hadn't relished being kicked all night in the confines of a single bed with him. Although perhaps she should think herself lucky she was sleeping in a bed at all tonight; she and Scott could so easily have ended up huddled together in the car somewhere.

She shrugged. 'If you're busy I can always...'

'Always what?' Jed Cole came back derisively, lounging in one of the armchairs but putting down the book he had been glancing through. 'Your choices are pretty limited in this cottage.'

A flush heightened her cheeks. She felt strangely uncomfortable now that she was alone with this darkly enigmatic man. Although he was only three, Scott's presence had acted as a buffer between the two adults, making personal conversation almost impossible. Something that was no longer true.

Especially after Scott's statement earlier concerning his grandparents.

And her parents, her whole family, in fact, were something she would rather not discuss.

She grimaced. 'Well, I could always go and tidy the kitchen.'

'All done,' Jed Cole dismissed dryly, almost as if he had guessed what she would do and had nullified it. 'For the main part the cottage is pretty basic, but it does have a dishwasher and washing machine, and, wonder of wonders, central heating.'

Meg had already noted that the entire cottage was warm, that the log fire burning in this room was only for effect and not to provide actual heat. 'Were they here when you bought the cottage or did you have them installed afterwards?' She moved further into the room, feeling slightly shy with this man, as shown by the inanity of her conversation.

Not surprising really. Jed Cole was the sort of darkly handsome man who would wreak havoc with any woman's pulse-rate at the best of times. Here, alone in a cottage with him, the snow on the ground outside creating an eerie silence, she found him nerve-janglingly attractive, his dark good looks, the intensity of his deep blue eyes, combined with the lean strength of his body, making Meg completely aware of him.

Which was quite an admission coming from a woman who hadn't so much as accepted a date in over three years.

Jed Cole shook his head now. 'I don't own the cottage, Meg, it belongs to…a friend of mine,' he dismissed abruptly. 'I've just been staying here for a while.'

Not exactly helpful. And she hadn't missed that slight pause when he'd told her whom the cottage belonged to. 'Do you work in the area?'

He settled back in the armchair, blue gaze hooded now. 'No.'

She gave him a quick glance, not sure whether or not to sit down herself; if they were going to continue this horribly stilted conversation, probably not. 'Perhaps you have friends in the area?'

He grimaced. 'Don't know a soul.'

Hmm, talkative man, wasn't he? Perhaps it would better if she just made her excuses and went back upstairs.

'My turn now,' Jed drawled hardly. 'Why has Scott never met your parents?'

She had known by the narrow-eyed way he'd looked at her at the time that he wasn't going to let that statement pass, but the directness of his question now threw her into some confusion. Most people, most polite people, wouldn't have pursued the subject, but Jed Cole had made no effort to be polite, so why should he start now?

'I was about to have a glass of red wine,' he continued lightly. 'Would you care to join me?'

Why not? She'd had a long and stressful day, and she somehow didn't think it was going to get too much better if Jed Cole was going to start asking her questions like the one he just had.

He stood up now, careful to avoid the dark wooden beams on the ceiling as he did so.

She should have known that he didn't own this cottage. It was like trying to fit a round peg into a square hole; he simply didn't fit.

'Perhaps you'll be able to think of an answer to my question while I go and get the wine,' he told her mockingly as they stood together in the doorway for several seconds.

Several seconds too long for Meg's comfort, her awareness of this man becoming more acute with every minute that passed. Which would never do. Despite what this man might think to the contrary, because she had Scott, she did not get involved in brief, meaningless affairs. Even with attractive men she met in snowstorms.

Neither did she have an acceptable answer to his question, she admitted with dismay. And his slightly mocking smile before he disappeared down the hallway to the kitchen seemed to say that he already knew she didn't.

Well, she did have an answer, but it wasn't one she could give without being unkind to her parents, and she didn't think they deserved that. It wouldn't have been easy for them to accept their daughter turning up on their doorstep with their illegitimate grandchild. Not that she ever had.

'Here we are.' Jed came back with two glasses and an opened bottle of red wine. 'Thought of an answer yet?' he taunted as he poured the wine into the two glasses before handing one to Meg. 'Why don't we sit down, hmm?'

If he was trying to put her at her ease, then he wasn't succeeding.

Although after one glance at his face, at those mockingly raised brows, she realized that perhaps he wasn't trying to do any such thing, that he was a man who rarely, if ever, tried to make things easy for other people. In fact, as Meg was quickly learning, he wasn't a man it was easy to relax around at all. And it didn't help that he was so sure of himself, that he wore his obviously expensive clothing with a complete disregard for their worth—or that he was so rakishly attractive.

Admit it, Meg, she mocked herself, it was the latter about him that bothered her the most. She was alone here, with only the sleeping Scott for chaperon, with a man it was impossible not to be completely physically aware of.

'Still trying to think of an answer?'

And who also happened to be purposefully blunt to the point of rudeness.

'We aren't usually this—inquisitive, into other people's personal lives, in this country.' She eyed him sternly, a look usually guaranteed to subdue Scott, but which only succeeded in making this somewhat older man smile.

He shrugged those broad shoulders unapologetically. 'These aren't usual circumstances.'

No, they weren't, were they? Because in the normal course of things single mothers like Meg wouldn't even be noticed by a man who was probably more at home with highly sophisticated New York types.

Which posed the question Scott had asked him earlier—why was he here and not in New York?

'In that case...' she paused to take a sip of her wine '...perhaps you wouldn't mind explaining to me—'

'Oh, no, little Meg,' he cut in tauntingly, totally relaxed as he watched her from beneath hooded lids. 'You've already asked enough questions for one evening. Or do you want me to repeat the question?'

'That won't be necessary,' she snapped tautly.

'I'm still waiting, Meg,' he prompted softly seconds later at her tight-lipped silence.

She was as disturbed by his use of her first name as she was by his persistence. Although it would be slightly ridiculous, given the circumstances, for them to continue to stand on formality.

This time her sip of wine was more from necessity than for effect. 'You would have to know my parents to understand.'

'Oh, I can believe that,' he drawled scathingly.

'My father has been ill.'

'How old is Scott?' he prompted hardly.

'Three and a half. But—'

'Your father has been ill for three and a half years?' he said disbelievingly.

'Of course not,' she snapped agitatedly. 'I was just… Our parents are in their sixties.'

'Our?' Jed picked up frowningly. 'You have siblings too?'

'One. A sister,' she supplied reluctantly, knowing that the sophisticated Sonia wouldn't have found herself blushing and stumbling in conversation with this wildly attractive man, that her sister would have known exactly what to do and say.

'Older or younger?' he prompted softly.

'Older. Just,' she added with a sigh, knowing she had succeeded in disconcerting him by the way his eyes widened.

'You have a twin sister?'

'No need to sound so surprised.' It was her turn to

mock him now. 'They say everyone has a lookalike some-where in the world, my sister just happens to be mine.'

He frowned. 'You're identical?'

'Yes,' she confirmed brightly. 'Or, at least, we were,' she added slowly.

'Either you are or you aren't,' Jed derided, obviously not one to be disconcerted for long.

'We are,' Meg confirmed abruptly. No need to mention that Sonia had had her teeth whitened and capped, the freckles on her nose minimized, and wore an all-year-round tan. 'But Sonia wears her hair short, and is—well, she's a lawyer. I'm the arty one.' She sighed. 'I'm an interior designer,' she explained as he seemed to be looking at her hands for signs of paint.

'Wow.' He gave a derisive smile as he looked around the room. 'You must be itching to change things in here.'

She wasn't sure she would know where to start.

Well, no, that wasn't strictly true, although the décor in here did run to worn and comfortable rather than elegant or eye-catching. She would take out all the heavy furniture for a start, replace it with—

'Just joking, Meg,' he drawled. 'As I told you, I don't own the place. As long as it has a chair for me to sit on and a bed for me to sleep in, I'm really not too inter-ested.' He sat forward in his armchair, cradling his glass of wine between long, sensitive hands. 'I am beginning to see a pattern emerging, though,' he told her softly.

Meg gave him a startled look. 'You are?'

'I am.' He gave a mocking inclination of his head. 'Twin girls, born to older parents, one twin practical and ambitious, the other more sensitive and artistic. The older twin goes on to make a successful career for herself as a lawyer, an advantageous marriage—she is married? I thought she might be,' he drawled at Meg's nod of confirmation. 'No kids, either, I suspect; plenty of time for that later, if at all. The younger twin, on the other hand, turned out to have an artistic flare, opted for art college in London rather than university before finally getting spat out into the real world, only to end up getting pregnant—'

'I think you have said quite enough, Mr Cole,' Meg cut in abruptly, turning away slightly so that he wouldn't see the sheen of tears in her eyes. 'It isn't polite to discuss people's personal lives in this way.'

'British reserve, you mean?' he derided. 'Yeah, I've heard of that. We have something like it in the States too. It's called respecting other peoples' privacy. But I seem to remember someone asking questions about my family before dinner.'

'It's hardly the same.' She turned sharply to snap at him, having brought those tears firmly under control. She had cried enough tears over the years over her family, without breaking down in front of this man.

Jed Cole looked up at her consideringly. 'Got a little too close to home, did I?'

Far too close. Although he hadn't been right about everything. No, not everything.

'Hey, don't beat yourself up about it,' Jed chided derisively. 'I'm the duckling in my nest of swans too: Granddad was a farmer, Dad's a farmer, my two brothers are farmers.'

'And you, Mr Cole, what exactly are you?' she challenged, still stung by their earlier conversation.

'Well, I sure as hell ain't a farmer,' he assured mockingly.

She already knew that, those strong, slender hands didn't grow crops or tend animals. In his youth maybe, but certainly not for the last twenty years or so.

He gave a confidently dismissive smile. 'We weren't discussing me.'

'We aren't discussing me, either.' Meg drank down some more of her wine before placing the almost empty glass down on the table. 'Offering Scott and I shelter for the night does not entitle you to comment on either myself or my family.'

'No?' he taunted huskily, putting his own glass down on the carpeted floor before getting slowly to his feet. 'Then what does it entitle me to?' he challenged, that vivid blue gaze moving over her slowly, from the tips of her toes to the top of her ebony head, before moving down slightly to rest speculatively on the fullness of her lips.

For some reason he was deliberately trying to unnerve her. And he was succeeding. The atmosphere between them was now charged with expectation, the intensity of his gaze almost tangible against her lips.

He was playing with her, Meg recognized frowningly. It was there in the mocking twist to his mouth, the hard gleam of laughter in his eyes.

She drew in an angry breath. 'It entitles you to my heartfelt thanks,' she bit out tautly.

He gave a brief inclination of his head. 'Which you've already made. Several times,' he drawled.

Her eyes sparkled with her anger. 'Which I've already made several times,' she agreed tightly. 'Now if you will excuse me.' She bent to pick her handbag up from the floor. 'It's been a long day, and I'm very tired.'

'Oh, I'll excuse you, Meg,' he told her mockingly. 'I'm sure that most men would excuse you anything.'

Her mouth tightened. 'Goodnight, Mr Cole,' she told him firmly before turning on her heel to leave.

''Night, Meg,' he called after her tauntingly.

Her shoulders stiffened slightly but she didn't halt her departure, only starting to breathe again once she was out in the hallway with the door firmly closed behind her.

Jed Cole was rude. He was hostile. He was mocking. He was, in a word, infuriating.

He was also one of the most handsome men she had ever seen. And far too sexy for his own good.

'Just exactly what do you think you're doing?'

Jed looked up to watch as a very irate Meg stomped across the snow towards them, her eyes sparkling deeply green, twin wings of angry colour in her cheeks.

Something had put a burr under her saddle, that was for sure, and it appeared to be him. Although he couldn't for the life of him think what he had done; this was the first time this morning that he had set eyes on her.

As to what he and Scott were doing, surely the two huge balls of snow, one placed on top of the other, the bottom one larger than the top, spoke for themselves.

But he was willing to humour her for the moment. 'We're building a snowman.'

'I can see that,' Meg snapped irritably. 'But don't you

think it would have been better to have woken me first and told me what you were doing?'

'Why?' Jed eyed her derisively. 'Did you want to build a snowman, too?' He folded his arms across his chest as he looked down at her.

'No, of course I—' she broke off her angry reply to glare at him frustratedly. 'You—'

'You really should have put a hat and coat on before coming out here,' Jed told her frowningly. She was already starting to shiver as the cold penetrated the red jumper and denims she wore. 'Especially as I made sure Scott was dressed appropriately before I would let him come outside.'

'Isn't our snowman great, Mummy?' The animated little boy was covered in enough snow to be a snowman himself, having insisted on rolling the huge balls of snow until they had become too heavy for him to move and Jed had had to take over. 'Jed says he has an old hat and scarf we can put on him.'

'Mr Cole, darling,' Meg corrected slightly distract-edly as she brushed some of the snow from his clothes.

Scott grimaced with what little of his face could be seen beneath the woollen hat and scarf he wore. 'But he said I could call him Jed, Mummy,' he dismissed with the simplicity of a child. 'Jed says we need a carrot and some coal, too, for his face.'

Jed watched the way Meg's mouth tightened slightly at this second 'Jed says' in as many minutes, sensing there was an explosion about to happen if he didn't in-tervene. 'How about Mummy and I go back into the cottage and get them right now?' he suggested lightly.

'You can look in the wood pile over there for some small branches that might do for arms, if you like,' he added as the little boy looked disappointed not to be included in the task.

'Cool!' Scott grinned before scampering off to the wood pile, totally impervious to the icy cold air that was now making his mother's teeth chatter.

Jed raised dark brows at a still frowning Meg. 'Shall we?' He indicated the cottage.

Her mouth firmed. 'I think we had better,' she muttered disgruntledly before turning and stomping back inside.

Jed followed at a more leisurely pace, sure that she wouldn't approve of the way he was watching her hips and backside move in the tight denims.

Yep, there was no doubt about it, Meg Hamilton was a fine-looking woman, under any circumstances. And Scott was a great little kid.

But they were also a complication he didn't need in his life, now or at any other time, so he had better stop thinking this way. Absolutely no involvement, he reminded himself sternly.

They got as far as the kitchen before she turned on him. 'I don't allow Scott to be overfamiliar with adults,' she told him stiffly.

'That's good.' He nodded tersely. 'I don't believe in being overfamiliar with adults, either.' Although he couldn't guarantee that was going to last too much longer where Meg was concerned. It was a cliché, he knew, but she really was beautiful when she was angry. Her eyes sparkled like emeralds, her cheeks were flushed, even her lips appeared redder. And more kissable.

'You know exactly what I.mean,' she told him frustratedly. 'And what do you mean by just disappearing outside with him in that way?' She stood hands on hips now as she challenged him.

'I don't see what your problem is.'

'My problem is that I woke up to find Scott gone, and neither of you to be found in the cottage.' She was tense with fury now. 'If I hadn't heard Scott laughing, and looked out of the window and seen you both I would have thought—'

'What?' he cut in icily. 'What would you have thought, Meg? That I had run off with him? Because if that thought even entered your mind I—'

'It didn't!' Her shocked expression said that it really hadn't. 'It was only that I woke up to find the bed beside me empty.'

'Always a disappointment,' he drawled, starting to relax again.

Meg shot him a reproving glare. 'Speaking for yourself, of course.'

'Oh, of course,' he murmured dryly.

'Humph.' She gave him a narrow-eyed look before continuing, 'Anyway, I woke up and Scott wasn't there. Neither were his clothes. A quick search of the cottage showed me that you weren't here, either. I thought—well, what I thought was that Scott must have woken up, been confused about where he was, and just—just wandered off somewhere. I thought you had gone after him. And that perhaps you had both got lost in the snow. And then I heard Scott laughing.' She choked back the tears. 'And when I looked out the window and saw the two of you happily building what I could clearly see was a snowman, well, that's when I got angry instead of scared.'

'And came straight out of the cottage ready to tear me limb from limb!' he drawled. 'You aren't becoming hysterical again, are you?' He eyed her warily; she was certainly babbling enough to be, had said more in the last five minutes than in the whole of their previous acquaintance. 'Because you know what I threatened to do the last time you became hysterical.' He could see by the sudden colour that flooded her cheeks that she did remember. Clearly.

'Of course I'm not becoming hysterical,' she defended strongly.

'No?' Well, there was no need for her to sound quite that certain. He wasn't sure it was good for his ego. His ego, be damned; women didn't usually make it so obvious they desperately wanted to avoid having him kiss them.

Now who was being irrational? Don't get involved, he had told himself. Firmly. Decisively. Now he felt annoyed that the woman he needed to keep his distance from also wanted to keep him at a distance.

'No,' she acknowledged agitatedly. 'I passed hysterical some time ago.'

'You did?' he grated speculatively.

'I did.' She nodded. 'And then I— What are you doing?' She gasped as he took hold of the tops of her arms. 'You don't need to shake me.' She looked up at him with guileless eyes. 'I told you, I was—' whatever she was or wasn't was cut off as Jed lowered his head and kissed her, something he had been wanting to do since last night.

Her lips felt soft and cool beneath his, but that

coolness was only from the cold outside, he quickly learnt as her mouth became warm and inviting.

It was all the encouragement he needed, his arms moving about the slenderness of her waist as he moulded her curves into his, her tiny hands coming to rest on his shoulders as she clung to him.

'Mummy, did you find the carrot and the—oh…'

Meg came to her senses a lot quicker than Jed did, obviously attuned to her son's voice, pulling sharply away to release herself and turn to where Scott stood in the doorway in open-mouthed fascination, his eyes huge green pools of curiosity.

'No, we haven't found them yet, Scott,' Meg's voice quivered slightly. 'We—I had something in my eye and Mr Cole, Jed, was getting it out for me,' she invented with a smoothness that had Jed staring at her too.

'Something in her eye' my eye, he glowered darkly. Although perhaps her version was better than telling Scott that Jed had been devouring his mother's mouth with a need that had quickly spiraled out of control.

So much for not getting involved.

What the hell had he been thinking?

He hadn't been thinking at all, that was the problem, only feeling. And Meg had felt very good indeed.

'The carrot's in the cool box in the fridge, and the coal is in the bucket in the sitting-room,' he rasped as Meg bent down so that her son could inspect that the imaginary something had definitely gone from her eye.

The face Meg turned towards him was white with strain. 'Where are you going?' she prompted huskily as Jed moved to the door.

'Out,' he barked harshly.

She blinked. 'Out where?'

'Just out!' he bit out tersely, making good his escape, having no real idea where he was going, only that he had to get away from Meg for a while.

And try to get the taste and feel of her out of his head.

CHAPTER FOUR

'THE main roads are clear if you would like to get your things together.'

Meg gave Jed a startled look as she sat at the table playing a game of cards with Scott, not having heard him come into the cottage.

Jed had been gone for over an hour, time enough for her to have helped Scott finish off the snowman, make him some breakfast and a cup of coffee for herself, before sitting down to play a game of Pairs with him.

But during all that time she had been half listening for the sound of Jed Cole's return, not quite knowing what to say to him after what had happened between them, the memory of that kiss still firmly in her mind, only knowing that she felt less alone when he was around.

Well, she was less alone when he was around, obviously. But it was more than that: there was an arrogant confidence about Jed, an assurance, that made her feel nothing could go too wrong while he was there.

Except that he might kiss her again, of course.

She had been too stunned earlier to do anything more

than respond when he'd started kissing her, and by the time she'd stopped feeling stunned she had found she was enjoying it too much to want it to stop.

Quite what to make of that, when she had only known the man for less than twenty-four hours, she wasn't quite sure. But it certainly made her feel shy about facing him again.

Except that now he was back he was telling her it was time for her and Scott to leave.

'You carry on playing, Scott,' she told her son softly. 'I just want to have a word with Mr—Jed,' she quickly amended as he scowled across the room at her.

She followed him out into the hallway as he stepped out of the room, firmly telling herself to forget what had happened between the two of them earlier, that it would be better for everyone if she did.

Except that she couldn't quite keep her gaze from the sensuous curve of his lips, or stop herself from remembering how they had felt against hers, or the slight abrasiveness of his chin, where he was in need of a shave, against the softness of hers.

'What word did you have in mind?' he drawled sarcastically. 'Opportunist? Lecher? Or maybe something worse?' He grimaced self-disgustedly.

'No, of course not,' she snapped impatiently. 'What happened earlier was the result of overheated emotions,' she dismissed with what she hoped was conviction, because she wasn't sure what it was the result of, only that she would never be able to forget it. 'You said we could leave? Does that mean I'll be able to phone the local garage, after all?'

'It means I've just walked down to the main road and back.'

'You have?' she gasped.

'I have,' he drawled. 'And pretty damn slippery it is, too. But I think I may be able to drive my Range Rover down the half a mile or so of this lane, and then the main road has been cleared, so I should be able to drive the two of you the rest of the way to your parents' house.'

Meg's eyes widened at this suggestion. 'I don't think that's a good idea at all,' she protested without thinking, a blush colouring her cheeks as his brows rose speculatively. 'I mean, I really can't put you to all that trouble.'

'And the alternative of having you and Scott remain here isn't putting me to any trouble?' he scorned.

Well, when he put it like that…!

'I wasn't meaning for us to remain here,' she came back sharply, accepting that she and Scott had probably been a nuisance to him since they arrived.

Although he had seemed to be getting on with Scott well enough earlier. That was before he had kissed her, Meg reminded herself, something he obviously deeply regretted if he was willing to attempt driving in the dangerous conditions to get rid of her.

She frowned. 'But if the main road is cleared now, perhaps I can order a taxi.'

'Will you get real, Meg?' Jed rasped his impatience. 'The half a mile down to the main road is almost suicidal, and even though the main road is cleared now, there is more snow forecast for later on today.'

'There is?' She groaned her dismay.

'There is,' he confirmed hardly. 'Now the way I look

at it is we have a small gap in the bad weather during which I can attempt to get you and Scott to your family in time for Christmas. Take it or leave it.'

She had to take it. Of course she did. Except that she was no longer in any hurry to get to her parents' house, not now that she knew that Sonia and Jeremy were going to be there too.

She swallowed hard. 'I don't want to put any of us in danger just for the sake of waiting a while.'

'Believe me, Meg, you're in more danger staying on here than we are attempting that ten-mile drive,' he rasped self-derisively.

What did he…? Surely he didn't mean…? He did, one look at those penetrating blue eyes told her.

'If you could transfer Scott's presents from my car to your Range Rover without Scott seeing you, I'll go and pack our things,' she told him evenly.

'I had a feeling you might,' Jed drawled, his throaty laugh following her up the stairs.

Well, she hadn't exactly handled that well, had she? Not that she had ever made a pretence of appearing cool and sophisticated; it simply wasn't her.

The fact that she had Scott, that all of her time the last three and a half years, when she hadn't been working, had been spent taking care of him, meant that she hadn't had much chance for a social life of her own, except the occasional cup of coffee with another young mother. Oh, she had dated before Scott was born, but she couldn't say any of those men had remotely prepared her for a man like Jed Cole.

If anyone could be prepared for a man like him.

He was older, more assured, probably a lot more experienced too, than any of the young men she had previously dated.

Not that she was dating Jed Cole, she mocked herself derisively. But she was attracted to him, had responded to his kiss, had felt a surge of pleasure at his touch, had no idea where that desire might have taken them if Scott hadn't interrupted them when he did.

But it was just as well that he had interrupted them now that Jed had offered to actually drive them to her parents' house.

Not an ideal arrangement, in itself. After the things she had already told him about her family, her mother's lack of interest, the fact that neither of her parents had ever met Scott, her twin sister Sonia, Meg didn't particularly want to introduce Jed to any of them. Something she would have no choice about once he had driven them to her parents' home. She could hardly expect him to just turn around and drive back to the cottage without so much as offering him a hot drink.

Oh, well, seeing as she had no choice in the matter anyway, perhaps it was a small price to pay for finally reaching her destination.

Although she wasn't quite so sure about that half an hour later as Jed struggled to keep the vehicle from sliding off the lane and into the hedgerow at its side, his face grim with concentration, Meg tense beside him as she sat in teeth-clenched silence, Scott the only one unconcerned by the danger—he had fallen asleep several minutes ago, obviously tired from his earlier exertions building the snowman.

But Meg understood now why Jed had been gone so long on his walk this morning, with drifts five feet high or so on some sides of the lane, only Jed's skilled driving keeping them from disaster.

In fact, she discovered shortly when Jed had turned the Range Rover onto the main road, she had kept her hands so tightly clenched during that hair-raising journey that she had imprints of her nails in the palms of her hands.

'Phew,' she breathed her relief, glad she didn't have to do that again.

Although the same couldn't be said for the man at her side, she knew, when he returned in a couple of hours or so.

'This is better, isn't it?' She relaxed slightly in the leather seat, actually able to see the road ahead now, huge piles of snow cleared to bank its edges.

No wonder she had got so lost the evening before.

'Slightly,' Jed muttered, his face pale from the strain of battling with the slippery lane.

Meg took the silence that followed as an indication that he didn't want to talk any more but concentrate on his driving.

She had no argument with that, couldn't think of anything to say, anyway, that wouldn't sound trite. Besides which, the nearer they got to the village of Winston, the more she could feel her own tension rising.

The truth was, she would have been so much happier remaining in London for Christmas, just Scott and herself, as it usually was. Added to which, she was sure her mother wouldn't have issued the invitation at all—

she hadn't any other year—if Meg's father hadn't recently been ill.

A heart attack.

Her father had suffered a heart attack two weeks ago, only a mild one according to her mother, but even so she hadn't let Meg know at the time, only telephoning her on Sunday with that news and the invitation.

She didn't understand her mother. Never had. Had always found her emotionally distant, her father by far the easiest of her two parents to relate to as she'd been growing up, although his job as a civil servant working in London had meant she'd really only seen him at the weekend, and once she and Sonia had gone to boarding-school at thirteen she hadn't even seen him then.

But if Sonia had been her mother's daughter, then Meg had definitely been her father's, and she had been deeply hurt that her mother hadn't bothered to let her know of his illness sooner. To which her mother had replied, 'There was nothing you could do, so there was no point in bothering you.'

She really was that duckling amongst swans that Jed had mentioned last night, had to admit that as a child she had sometimes wondered if they could possibly be her real family at all; if not for her twin she would se-riously have doubted it.

'We're entering Winston now,' Jed told her grimly some time later. 'You'll have to give me directions from here.'

Meg felt her nervous tension return as she told him to turn right out of the town, a fluttering sensation in her stomach at what lay ahead.

For Scott's sake this visit had to go well, and she was

more than willing to play her part, if only she could be sure the rest of the family would do the same. Because if they didn't, this could be a very short visit indeed.

'Here?' Jed rasped incredulously as she told him to turn into the driveway to the left.

'Yes,' she confirmed woodenly, deliberately not looking at him, knowing he couldn't help but notice the grandeur of the imposing house and grounds they were now approaching down a driveway that had been totally cleared of snow.

But even though she wasn't looking at him she could feel Jed's narrowed gaze on her for several long seconds, probably wondering how this single mother, with a hire car for transport—a damaged hire car that the company had agreed to have towed away as soon as the weather cleared, and only a holdall with her own and Scott's clothes in for their short stay, could possibly come from a family of such obvious wealth.

She might even have found his incredulity funny if she didn't feel quite so nervous about facing them all again.

Oh, she heard from Sonia from time to time, as both of them lived in London, awkward conversations where they said nothing of any importance. She had even met her sister for coffee once or twice while Scott had been at playschool—all right, once!—but she couldn't claim that either of them had enjoyed the experience, too much between them left unsaid.

And their lifestyles were so totally different, Sonia with her socialite friends and showcase house, and Meg with her other young-mother friends and often untidy apartment, so they weren't likely to meet socially either.

She could feel Jed's gaze on her again, so intense now it was impossible to withstand.

'What?' she prompted irritably.

'This is where you were brought up?' he rasped disbelievingly.

Meg looked out the window as the house loomed closer, a huge four-storey mansion in mellow stone that was bigger than the whole building she lived in, and that housed eight flats.

'Yes,' she confirmed heavily. 'Look,' she continued irritably as his silence seemed brooding, 'my mother was a Winston before she married my father. The Winstons had the manor here for generations, the village is named for them, then they built this house a couple of hundred years ago.' She was babbling again, she knew she was, but Jed's silence made her feel uncomfortable. 'My mother was an only child, and so when her parents died she inherited.'

'Was it lonely living out here so far away from the rest of the village?' Jed frowned as he looked round at the bleak, unpopulated landscape.

'Yes,' she confirmed huskily, 'apart from Sonia, it was very lonely.' Once again this man had surprised her with his perception.

Because he had guessed perfectly last night when he'd talked of the older and younger twin, and now, instead of envying her this obviously privileged background, he was commenting on how lonely it must have been.

She blinked back the sudden tears caused by his understanding of the situation. 'Wasn't it lonely on your parents' farm?'

'With two younger brothers and too many cousins to count?' He snorted dismissively.

It sounded wonderful to Meg, the sort of childhood she would have wished for Scott but knew he would never have.

Jed was still scowling as he brought the Range Rover to a halt in front of the house. 'No wonder you decided not to come back here to bring Scott up.'

Meg gave a brief, humourless laugh. 'Believe me, it was never an option.' Her mother barely managed to remember Scott's birthday, and when she did the gift was usually a cheque pushed inside his card, very useful to a child of three.

Jed's mouth tightened. 'I don't think I'm going to like your mother very much.'

She wasn't sure her mother was going to like him, either. There was only room for one bluntly autocratic person in the Hamilton household, and her mother was definitely it.

She gave a rueful smile. 'You don't have to stay too long,' she assured sympathetically. 'In fact, if you would rather not go in at all I shall perfectly understand.' Although strangely, after previously wishing Jed didn't have to meet any of her family, now that they were here she was reluctant to see him go. His bluntness was preferable by far to the cold lack of welcome she knew she would find within.

'Are you kidding?' he came back scathingly as he switched off the ignition. 'I wouldn't miss this for anything.'

Meg wasn't quite sure she trusted that glint of challenge she could detect in those deep blue eyes, but, to be honest, she was too grateful not to be entering the lion's den on her own after all to question his motives.

'Is this Granma and Grandad's house, Mummy?' Scott had predictably woken up at the soothing throb of the engine being switched off.

She turned to give him a reassuring smile. 'It certainly is, darling.'

His eyes were wide as he looked up at the imposing house. 'It's big, Mummy,' he said uncertainly.

'It won't look half as big once you're inside,' she said with more hope than conviction.

Perhaps she should have tried to prepare Scott more for this meeting with her family, but how did you even start to explain to a three-year-old that his grandmother could be a cold autocrat, that his grandfather was too mild to stop her, and that his aunt Sonia—Meg didn't even know how to begin to tell him about his aunt Sonia.

She would just have to hope that the subtle nuances of any adult conversation would go way over his innocent head.

As it was she approached the wide oak front door with all the enthusiasm of the condemned man approaching the block.

'Cheer up, Meg,' Jed encouraged teasingly, obviously feeling no such trepidation as he moved lightly up the steps beside her. 'It may never happen.'

He had no idea.

'You ring the doorbell of your own parents' home?' he questioned incredulously as she did exactly that.

'Well…yes.' She grimaced, sure things were much more relaxed on his parents' farm.

He really didn't have any idea.

She could hear the click of heels on the hall tiles now, her hand tightening involuntarily about Scott's as she prepared herself to face her mother.

'Sonia, I didn't expect you back just yet—' Her mother's voice dried to a halt as, having opened the door fully, she realized her mistake. 'Margaret.' She frowned at Meg. 'I thought you were going to ring me and let me know when you were arriving?' She looked down her patrician nose.

'I was. I should have.' But she had totally forgotten that promised telephone call in the rush of leaving the cottage.

Not that her mother had needed the warning to correct any defects in her appearance. As usual her mother looked perfect, her dark hair styled, her make-up and lipstick applied, the cream cashmere sweater she wore with a black skirt perfectly tailored to her slim figure.

Meg glanced awkwardly at Jed, shaking her head slightly as he mouthed 'Margaret?' at her, a name she had detested since childhood, deciding at eight, after reading *Little Women*, that she wanted to be called Meg instead; only her mother refused to use it.

'There wasn't time,' she apologized awkwardly as she turned back to her mother. 'I didn't think—'

'The oversight was my fault, I'm afraid, Mrs Hamilton,' Jed cut in smoothly as he moved forward slightly to make his presence known.

If he was expecting that to change her mother's

demeanour he was in for a disappointment, Meg thought with a wince as her mother's gaze moved past her to Jed Cole, those eyes only becoming more coldly blue, her expression more frosty, if that were possible.

God, this was awful. Worse than she could possibly have imagined. She should never have come. Wished the ground would open up and swallow her.

Instead, as if programmed, she made the introductions. 'Jed, this is my mother, Lydia Hamilton. Mother, this is—'

'Jerrod, Jerrod Cole,' he cut in harshly as he took the limpness of her mother's hand in his much larger one. 'It's a pleasure to meet you, Lydia,' he added derisively.

And no wonder, Meg frowned, a transformation having come over her mother's face, the coldness fading from her eyes to be replaced with incredulity, a slight paleness to her perfectly defined cheekbones.

'I…' her mother swallowed, looking at Jed uncertainly now, as if she weren't quite sure of herself. 'Do you mean the Jerrod Cole who wrote *The Puzzle*?'

'Of course no—'

'I'm flattered that you've heard of me, Lydia,' Jed cut smoothly across Meg's denial.

Meg stared at him disbelievingly.

Jerrod Cole.

Jed was Jerrod Cole?

Well, of course her mother had heard of Jerrod Cole; probably the whole of the western world had heard of him. His book, *The Puzzle*, had been at the top of the best-seller lists for the last nine months, a film of the book was already in production.

But Jed couldn't be that Jerrod Cole.

Could he?

He really hadn't meant to just dump the truth on Meg like that. Margaret? She didn't look anything like a Margaret. He hadn't intended telling her he was Jerrod Cole at all. But Lydia Hamilton's attitude towards her youngest daughter had infuriated him so much he had just wanted to wipe that self-satisfied coldness from her unwelcoming face. And telling her exactly who he was had seemed the best way to do that.

He had never actually disliked anyone on sight before; usually it took him at least ten minutes or so. But Lydia Hamilton's behaviour towards Meg, the way she hadn't even looked at Scott, her own grandson, just made him want to shake the woman. And telling her his identity had certainly done that.

Although a quick glance at Meg showed him that she was as stunned by who he was as her mother, also that she wasn't at all happy with this development, staring at him now as if she had never seen him before.

Which, in fact, she hadn't. Not as Jerrod Cole, anyway.

But, damn it, Meg hadn't recognized him when she'd come to the cottage, and, considering anonymity was the reason he was staying at the cottage in the first place, he wasn't going to go around advertising the fact he was the author Jerrod Cole, now was he?

Although somehow, as a glitter of anger started to

show in Meg's eyes, he didn't think she was going to be too impressed with that explanation.

He abruptly released Lydia Hamilton's hand. 'Although I would really rather you just thought of me as a friend of Meg's,' he added smoothly.

'A friend of…yes, of course,' Lydia looked completely flustered at this stage.

'Perhaps you would like to invite us inside, Lydia?' He spoke hardly now. 'It's getting a little wet out here.' He looked pointedly at the snow that had just started to fall again, landing on their bare heads before melting.

'Of course.' She stepped back so that they could enter.

Which, after another frowning glance in his direction, Meg did, Scott's hand still tightly clenched in hers.

Jed's anger towards Lydia Hamilton turned to cold fury as he looked at the slightly bewildered little boy.

How could she remain so indifferent to such a cute kid? He knew he hadn't been able to earlier this morning when Scott had begged to go outside and make a snowman. Scott looked so exactly like his mother, and surely, somewhere behind that cold mask, Lydia Hamilton loved her youngest daughter.

Maybe not, he decided after another hard glance at the older woman.

Aged in her early sixties, Lydia Hamilton was one of those women who looked as perfect first thing in the morning as she did last thing at night, never a hair out of place, her make-up applied expertly so as to smooth out any lines, the skirt and sweater she wore ultra-smart. Jed somehow couldn't imagine this woman ever getting down on the floor to play with her children the way that Meg did with Scott.

Although she was fast recovering from her surprise, her smile once again cool. 'Please come through to the sitting-room, Mr Cole, and meet my husband, David.'

'Hey, look, Scott, a Christmas tree.' Jed, having detected a slight trembling to the little boy's bottom lip, moved quickly forward to pick him up in his arms and carry him across the cavernous hallway to look at the decorated tree, the urge inside him to actually strangle Lydia for her insensitivity to her grandson firmly held in check. He didn't think Meg would appreciate it if he were to murder her mother in front of her eyes.

Scott cheered up at the sight of the nine-feet-high decorated tree, his eyes soon shining bright with wonder as he gazed at all the meticulously applied decorations and lights.

Relieved that his distraction had worked, Jed was nevertheless aware of the conversation taking place across the hallway between the two women.

'I think you might have told me, Margaret,' Lydia Hamilton snapped softly. 'I felt ridiculous not knowing who the man was.'

Jed would take a bet on Meg feeling something a little stronger than ridicule.

But he didn't regret what he had done for a moment. It had been worth it just to see the cold arrogance wiped off Lydia Hamilton's face.

Meg took her time answering her mother, seeming to choose her words carefully when she did speak, 'Jed likes to keep his anonymity for the main part,' she finally responded huskily.

'Well, yes, I can understand that, but—what are we going to do with him?' Lydia Hamilton sounded flustered again—not a frequent occurrence, Jed would hazard a guess.

'Why, nothing.' Meg sounded startled by the question. 'Jed isn't going to—'

'Lydia, who was that at the door? Meg!'

Jed had put Scott down to turn at the first sound of that masculine voice, just in time to see the pleasure that lit the paleness of Meg's face before she launched herself at the man who had to be her father, a tall, thin man with eyes as green as his daughter's.

'Daddy.' Meg choked emotionally as she hugged her father tightly.

'Daddy', not the formal 'Mother' with which she spoke to Lydia Hamilton, Jed noted with satisfaction, glad there was one person in this household, at least, who was pleased to see Meg. Although that relief was short-lived as he remembered that this man was just as guilty of neglecting his daughter and grandson the last three and a half years as his wife was.

He looked critically at the older man. David Hamilton was still a handsome man, his hair white, with a definite look of Meg about him in the eyes and face, although that face showed the pale unhealthiness of a recent illness, his sweater and trousers seeming slightly too big for his frame too, as if he had recently lost weight.

The illness had been a recent thing, then, Jed decided.

Perhaps the reason Lydia seemed to have relented where her youngest daughter was concerned? It would be too much to hope that it had been for Meg and Scott's sakes.

Jed glanced down as Scott tugged at his trouser leg, going down on his haunches as he saw the little boy was looking shyly at the man his mother was hugging.

'Is that man my grandad, Jed?' he prompted in what he no doubt thought was a hushed voice, but nonetheless which carried in the cavernous hallway.

David Hamilton stiffened slightly before putting Meg slowly away from him and turning to look at the source of that voice.

Jed's move was purely instinctive as he placed a protective hand on Scott's shoulder. Lydia Hamilton's complete indifference to her grandson had been hard enough to witness; Jed felt as if he might actually do someone physical harm—even a recently ill man—if David Hamilton were to hurt the boy too.

'Yes, Scott, I'm your granddad.' David Hamilton spoke gently, his gaze riveted on Scott's small features as he slowly walked over to where they stood. 'Goodness, you look just like your mummy did at your age,' he breathed emotionally, a glitter of tears in those faded green eyes as he bent down to the little boy's level.

'Do I?' Scott breathed excitedly. 'Do I really?'

'You certainly do,' his grandfather assured him huskily. 'Why don't you come with me and I'll show you some photographs of her that I keep in my study?' He held out his arms, earning Jed's approval as he let the little boy come to him rather than forcing the issue.

'David, I don't think you should be exerting—'

'I'm perfectly fine, Lydia,' David cut in harshly on his wife's protest, his gaze still on his grandson. 'Scott?' His voice gentled again as he encouraged the little boy to come to him.

Jed glanced across at the two women who stood together watching this scene, Meg with tears of happiness shining brightly in her eyes, Lydia's expression much harder to read, although Jed thought he recognized concern there. For her husband, he guessed, so perhaps the woman did have some redeeming qualities, after all. Somewhere behind that coldness.

Scott, he was pleased to see, had responded to his grandfather's gentleness, and was now securely held in the man's arms as David straightened and looked at Jed for the first time, as if just noticing him. Which, considering the emotional reconciliation the man had just had with his daughter, his first ever meeting with his grandson, he probably hadn't, Jed acknowledged ruefully.

The older man gave him a quizzical look. 'Jerrod Cole, isn't it?' He held out his free hand in welcome.

'It is.' Jed shook that hand, finding the grip firm. 'But I would prefer it if you called me Jed,' he added lightly.

'And I'm David.' The older man smiled. 'I enjoyed your book very much. Can't wait for the next one to come out.'

That had the effect of wiping the smile off Jed's face. 'I'm working on it, thank you, sir.'

'David, please,' the older man insisted. 'I've had a lot of time for reading recently,' he added ruefully.

'David, how on earth did you know that Margaret's friend is Jerrod Cole?' Lydia prompted with hard suspicion.

Her husband gave her a level glance. 'I recognize him from the photograph on the back of his book, of course,' he dismissed mildly before turning back to Jed. 'I take it you can actually pilot the plane you're standing next to?' he teased.

Jed easily returned that smile. 'I can.'

'Good.' The older man nodded. 'I'll take this young man and show him those photographs now.' He bestowed a warm smile on the patiently waiting Scott.

'I'll come with you,' his wife put in quickly.

'That really isn't necessary, Lydia,' David assured her lightly, but the slight edge in his tone brooked no argument. 'Why don't you take Meg and Jed through to the sitting-room and offer them a drink?' he softly, but again firmly, reminded his wife of her manners.

It was easy to see by the bright wave of colour in Lydia's cheeks as her husband departed with Scott that she wasn't at all happy with this arrangement, but at the same time recognized that she had no choice but to comply.

'Margaret, why don't you take Mr—Jed, through to the sitting-room and I'll go and organize some refreshments before lunch?' She didn't wait for an answer but moved off stiffly down the hallway.

Jed had been studiously avoiding looking at Meg for the last few minutes, first because he had felt like something of an intruder to that emotional reunion with her father, and after that because he had been able to feel the accusation in her gaze as she'd looked at him, obviously none of what had happened in the last few minutes detracting from her earlier anger at his duplicity. Something he knew he was likely to hear about now that they were alone.

Yep, the sparkle in her eyes, the firmness of her mouth, told him he was definitely going to hear about it.

He sighed. 'Meg, why don't you hear me out before you say what you're obviously bursting to say?'

'You're Jerrod Cole,' she accused impatiently, as if that nullified anything else he might have to say in his defence.

'Well, yes, I am aware of that.' He grimaced. 'But I'm also Jed Cole. And it was Jed Cole that you met yesterday—'

'They're one and the same person,' she interrupted irritably.

'No, not really.' He sighed. 'I—' He broke off as the front door suddenly swung open behind them, a gust of cold air and snow preceding the two people who entered.

A tiny woman wearing a long white luxurious coat and matching hat, her face flushed from the cold as she laughed huskily at something her companion was saying.

The man was tall and grey-haired, his handsome face lined beside nose and mouth, teeth very white against his tan as he grinned down at the woman, limping very slightly as he moved to close the door.

Obviously Meg's brother-in-law, Jeremy.

Which meant the woman had to be her sister, Sonia.

The woman had removed her hat now, moving slender, perfectly manicured fingers through the short dark tresses, green eyes narrowing, her smile slowly fading, as she turned and saw that they weren't alone.

There were no impish freckles on her nose, and she didn't have that slightly overlapping tooth to the left of her front teeth, either, but even so Jed recognized her as Meg's twin, Sonia.

Identical, and yet strangely not so, just as Meg had tried to tell him.

And that tall, distinguished man at her side, a man surely old enough to be her father, was her husband, Jeremy.

Jed's gaze shifted to Meg, and he took an instinctive step closer to her as he saw how pale she had become. He wasn't exactly sure why—this was her twin sister, after all—but offering her his support, anyway.

So much for not getting involved—he was involved up to his thirty-eight-year-old neck.

CHAPTER FIVE

Meg felt as if she were somehow frozen in time, as if everything were happening in slow motion.

First that frosty meeting with her mother, then that startling revelation about Jed—a revelation, no matter what he might wish to the contrary, that she hadn't finished talking to him about.

He was Jerrod Cole, for goodness' sake.

She still couldn't quite believe it.

The man had become a publishing phenomenon this last year, the sale of his book *The Puzzle*—what an apt title for such an enigmatic man—outselling anything that had come before it, on both sides of the Atlantic. The film rights had been sold for a record amount of money too.

Meg read the newspapers, but she hadn't yet found the time to buy and read the book everyone was talking about.

Something she should maybe rectify now that she had actually met the author.

Then had come that emotional reunion with her father. An older, thinner, strangely different father.

She couldn't quite say in what way he was different,

only that he was. Maybe because of his heart attack, or maybe for some other reason she wasn't aware of.

Not that he had been any different with her, just his usual loving self. And she couldn't have asked for a better response from him towards Scott.

There was just something not quite right, an unspoken strain between him and her mother, perhaps? Meg had certainly never heard him speak to her mother in quite that firm tone before.

But this unexpected—until last night when she'd spoken to her mother on the telephone—meeting with her sister was certainly an added strain Meg could well have done without.

They had been close once, very close, but time, and circumstances, had ensured that was no longer the case.

Sonia looked no more pleased about the two of them being here together as their gazes met in silent battle. An antagonism in Sonia's face that she quickly masked as she realized they weren't alone, her gaze shifting slightly sideways to where Jed stood at Meg's side, those green eyes widening slightly, not in recognition, Meg didn't think, but rather a female response to an attractive man.

Meg couldn't even bring herself to glance in Jed's direction to see what his reaction was to this sleeker, more sophisticated version of herself.

'Meg, darling.' Sonia finally spoke with bright brittleness. 'How lovely to see you here.' She crossed the room to give Meg a brief hug, touching cheeks, her kiss floating away in the air. 'And this is…?' She gave Jed a look of frankly female appreciation.

Meg fought down the instinct to gnash her teeth together as she easily interpreted that speculative glance for what it was, instead making the introductions as briefly as possible, including Jeremy as he strolled over to join them, favouring his left leg slightly as he did so.

Sonia, unlike their mother a short time ago, received Jed's identity with a few complimentary comments about his book and a narrow-eyed glance in Meg's direction.

No doubt her sister was wondering how Meg, of all people, had managed to meet such a famous and fascinating man.

'And where is little—Scott, I believe you called him?' Sonia prompted with a noticeable coolness in her voice.

Meg drew in a sharp breath, the abrupt reply she was about to make forestalled by her mother's return.

'I'm so glad you managed to get back before the storm started again,' she said evenly as she saw that her eldest daughter and son-in-law had now joined them.

'Only just,' Sonia drawled ruefully. 'If you'll all excuse us while we go upstairs and freshen up before lunch?' she added to no one in particular, taking hold of her husband's arm as the two of them went up the stairs together.

'It's snowing heavily again?' Meg prompted with dismay. How on earth was Jed going to get back to the cottage if that were the case.

'Worse than yesterday,' her father answered as he returned with Scott still in his arms, her son, Meg was pleased to see, more than happy with the arrangement. 'I should go and get your luggage from the car now, Jed, while you still have your outdoor clothes on, before it gets any worse.'

'Oh, but—'

'Good idea, David.' Jed spoke firmly. 'Coming with me, Meg?' he added purposefully.

She looked up at him frowningly. First he announced he was a friend of hers, and now he was proposing they get their luggage from the Range Rover. But he didn't have any luggage. Did he?

She gave a puzzled shake of her head. 'But wouldn't you be better—?'

'I can't carry it all on my own,' he told her teasingly. 'I think she packed enough things to stay for a month,' he confided in her father.

Meg's frown only deepened at this comment. Because Jed knew how untrue that was, had already commented himself on the small amount of luggage she had brought with her. Although there were all of Scott's Christmas presents, of course.

However, there were still a few things she would like to say to Jed—Jerrod Cole—in private.

But apparently there were a few things he had to say to her too. 'Phew,' he breathed in relief once they were safely outside with the front door firmly closed behind them. 'No wonder you were in no rush to get here.' He grimaced. 'Your dad seems okay, but as for the rest of them.' He shook his head. 'Your mother is like a reversed iceberg—the ice is ninety per cent above the surface rather than the other way around,' he explained ruefully at Meg's questioning look. 'Your sister I haven't worked out yet, except that she seems to be married to a man twice her age. Although he seems okay too, so maybe it's only the female members of the family who are a bit odd.'

Meg had stared at him incredulously through this monologue about her family, totally immune to the fresh snow buffeting and gusting about them. 'Do I take it that I'm included in that last sweeping statement?'

Jed grinned unabashedly. 'Oh, no, in comparison, you're quite normal.'

'You're so kind.' Sarcasm dripped off her voice.

His grin widened. 'Come on.' He grabbed her arm. 'Let's go and sit in the Range Rover out of the snow, I'm sure there are a few things you would still like to say to me.' He gave her a mocking glance.

'Oh, just a few,' she agreed as the two of them ran down the front steps to get in the Range Rover, at once feeling warmer as the wind continued to howl outside. 'Jerrod Cole?' she prompted again pointedly.

'Yeah.' He grimaced. 'I usually like to keep quiet about that.'

'Well, in my case, you succeeded,' she assured him disgustedly, still feeling rather foolish for not having recognized him.

Although, in all honesty, not many of the reports of the success of *The Puzzle* had actually included a photograph of the author, and those that had been included were black and white and quite grainy to look at, and Jed's hair had been much shorter, too.

Besides, in her defence, a tiny cottage in the middle of the English countryside was the very last place she would have expected to meet the amazingly successful American author, Jerrod Cole.

'You might have told me,' she said exasperatedly. 'I felt, feel, like such a fool for not recognizing who you were.' The man was a writing phenomenon and he had been out in the snow this morning with her son building a snowman.

God, that seemed like such a long time ago. In fact, part of her, a large part of her, wished she were still back there.

'Then don't,' Jed grated. 'The truth is I wasn't going to tell you at all, was going to deliver you and Scott here, make polite conversation for a short time, and then leave. That is, until I met your mother.' His voice hardened over the latter.

'My mother?' Meg frowned her puzzlement with this statement.

He nodded. 'I didn't like the way she spoke to you.'

'I'm used to it.' Meg shrugged.

'And ignored Scott.' His voice was icy now. 'Even if she disapproves of the fact that you have him, although in this day and age even that's ridiculous, she had absolutely no right to just ignore him like that.' His expression was grim. 'It may not be very commendable, but I wanted, if only briefly, to wipe that haughty look off her face.'

Oh, he had succeeded in doing that all right. He had succeeded in stunning Meg too.

'And what's with the "Margaret" thing?' he continued scathingly. 'You obviously prefer to be called Meg, the rest of the family call you Meg, so why not your own mother?'

'I don't know,' Meg admitted dully. 'Maybe…' She broke off, staring down at her ringless hands.

'What?' Jed prompted shrewdly.

She shrugged. 'Maybe it's too familiar. I don't know.'

She had never known, had never been able to understand why, as a child, she had received hugs and kisses from her father, but not from her mother. Not that Sonia had fared any better in that direction, but it had never seemed to bother her sister as much as it did her; Sonia and their mother were very alike in that respect, emotionally self-contained.

As a child Meg had wished she could be more like them, but as an adult she was very glad that she wasn't.

She wouldn't have been able to be the warm and loving mother to Scott that she was if that were the case.

She wouldn't have enjoyed Jed kissing her as much this morning, if she were, wouldn't, even now, be wondering what it would be like to kiss him again.

Despite what she now knew about his identity, Jed was still the only breath of security in a very unusual situation.

'Familiar sounds fine to me,' he said huskily.

Meg gave him a startled look, her pulse starting to beat more rapidly as she noticed how close he was in the confines of the Range Rover, her gaze easily caught and held by the intense blue of his.

'Admit it, Meg,' Jed murmured softly. 'You were secretly relieved at the way I diverted your mother's attention from you onto me,' he explained as she gave him a guarded look.

Oh, that. For a moment there she had thought he knew, had guessed, she was too attracted to him for her own good, which would be just too embarrassing in the circumstances.

But he was perfectly correct about her relief earlier; her mother really was hard work.

'I'm not so sure about the "just think of me as a friend of Meg's" remark.' She gave him a reproving look, hoping that nothing she was saying or doing was betraying how totally aware she was of him.

He grinned unabashedly. 'Would you rather I had told your mother I'm just the man you picked up in a snowstorm?'

Meg drew in a sharp breath, even while inwardly she admitted, within very wide guidelines, that he spoke the truth.

She glared at him. 'I'll be more than happy to put you down again!'

'In this weather?' He glanced out at the heavily falling snow. 'There's gratitude for you.' Even as he shook his head reprovingly his eyes were laughing at her.

One thing was becoming more and more apparent to her by the second: the snow falling steadily outside was such that Jed was never going to make it back to the cottage today.

'Do you really have some luggage with you?' She frowned. 'Or did you just make that up?'

He grimaced. 'I have an overnight bag with me. I never thought I was going to get back to the cottage today, Meg,' he added as her eyes widened at the admission. 'There's a hotel in Winston; I was going to try and book in there for the night.'

There was no way she could allow him to do that after all that he had done for her and Scott. And if he wasn't to stay in a hotel tonight, then he would have to stay here.

He was so close to her now, the weather cocooning them in a world of silence, that at that moment nothing else seemed to exist but the two of them, the very air between them seeming electrified with expectation.

As if becoming aware of that himself, Jed's eyes darkened, his narrowed gaze moving down to the parted softness of her lips.

Meg instinctively moistened those lips with the tip of her tongue.

'I really can't let you do that.' She didn't get any further, staring up at Jed in fascination as he looked down at her only briefly before lowering his head, his mouth easily capturing hers.

It was as if the time since earlier this morning had never been, her lips parting beneath his as he deepened the kiss, pulling her into his arms, although the stowing box between them stopped them getting as close as Meg would have liked. Wanted. Desired.

His hair felt so thick and silky against her fingers, heat building inside her as she met the fiery passion of his kiss.

A blast of cold air gusted inside the Range Rover as the door beside Meg was wrenched open, Meg pulling away self-consciously from Jed to turn and look at her brother-in-law, Jeremy's teasing expression telling her he knew exactly what he had just interrupted.

'The two of you have been gone so long Lydia sent me out to make sure you hadn't somehow got lost in the snow,' Jeremy drawled, smiling, seemingly impervious to the falling snow.

She had only met Jeremy twice, once when he'd come to the flat one evening to pick her sister up for a date, and the second time when the two of them had told her they were engaged to be married, but on both occasions she had rather liked him.

Although she wasn't too sure she liked the fact that

he had caught her and Jed—well, in an embarrassing situation if not a compromising one.

'Lydia did? Or was it David?' Jed was the one to respond to the other man sceptically.

Jeremy gave him a rueful smile. 'Oh, it was definitely Lydia—her tea is getting cold, I'm afraid.'

Meg watched as the two men shared what could only be classed a male understanding look.

How did Jed do that? Meg wondered with some bewilderment. He had quite effortlessly silenced her mother earlier, immediately charmed her father, remained totally immune to Sonia's sensual charm, and now he and Jeremy were exchanging looks like conspirators in a war.

Jed's mouth twisted ruefully. 'Please tell Lydia we'll be right in,' he drawled dryly.

Jeremy turned to give Meg a friendly smile. 'You're looking really well, Meg,' he told her warmly before closing the door to return to the house.

The implication being that the way she looked had something to do with having Jed Cole in her life.

She shot him a glance. 'We really will have to stop doing that.'

'Will we?' he mused softly. 'Why?'

'Because…well…' she frowned as she pushed back the heavy curtain of her hair '…two strangers caught in a snowstorm together and all that.'

'We're hardly alone, Meg,' he mocked pointedly. 'And I don't think we can be called strangers any more, either,' he added teasingly.

No, they weren't, were they? she accepted a little

dazedly as they got out of the Range Rover to collect the luggage from the back. But she would be a fool to read more into a couple of kisses than there really was. Because as soon as the snow cleared Jed would be on his way. Back to New York, probably. And she would never see him again.

Don't, for goodness' sake, get involved, Meg, she told herself firmly as she helped carry the luggage inside.

At the same time having the feeling her warning might have come too late.

Jed knocked on the door to Meg's room, waiting for her to answer, and when she didn't he opened the door and went inside anyway, sure that she was in there.

She was, lying on one of the single beds, an arm up and draped over her eyes, Scott already fast asleep in the other bed, angelically beautiful, a large red sack draped over the bottom of the bed.

Jed padded softly across the room on bare feet, intending—well, he didn't know what he intended doing, only that he was drawn to these two like a magnet. He wasn't sure what that meant, either.

'It's far too early for Father Christmas,' Meg murmured without moving the arm from over her eyes.

'Damn it, woman, you startled me. I thought you must have fallen asleep,' he said irritably as she shifted her arm slightly to look at him.

'No,' she assured him flatly. 'I'm certainly not asleep.'

Jed stood next to the bed looking down at her. 'Then what are you doing?'

She sighed, her arm falling back to her side, her eyes

closed now. 'I'm lying here trying not to scream. What are you doing?' she demanded with some alarm as he moved to stretch out on the bed beside her.

He lay back with his eyes closed. 'The same as you—trying not to scream. That has got to be the weirdest afternoon I've ever spent. Are you usually that polite to each other?' His own family was noisy and boisterous, a row usually breaking out between a couple of them within minutes of their meeting up again.

'Usually, yes.' Meg frowned.

He gave a disgusted shake of his head. 'And who changes for dinner when it's just family?' he continued disbelievingly, having known himself dismissed a short time ago when the whole family had risen to go upstairs to their respective bedrooms to change for dinner.

Except Meg, of course. She had escaped over an hour ago after giving Scott his tea in the kitchen, coming back to announce, much to Scott's disappointment, that it was now time for his bath before going to bed.

When Meg hadn't returned after an hour Jed had been sure that she must have fallen asleep too, this the first opportunity he'd had to check up on her.

He opened one eye at Meg's continued silence after his last statement, only to find she had propped herself up on one elbow and was now looking at him. 'What?' he asked tersely.

She shook her head, turning away slightly. 'You shouldn't be in here,' she told him quietly.

'Why shouldn't I? We're more than adequately chaperoned.' He gave a pointed look at the sleeping Scott. 'Although I didn't get the impression earlier that would be such a problem, anyway,' he drawled as he turned back to look at Meg. A blushing Meg. 'You should have seen your face earlier when your mother asked if we would be sharing a room.' He had found it difficult at the time to contain his humour at the look of shock on Meg's face; now he gave a teasing grin at the memory.

Although he had to admire the dignity with which Meg had informed her mother that she and Scott would be sharing a bedroom, not Meg and Jed.

But Lydia had still allocated them adjoining rooms, with a communicating door between, the doorway he had just come through.

Meg shook her head impatiently, her face pale. 'I can't imagine what my mother was thinking of!'

Jed raised dark brows. 'Possibly treating you like the adult you obviously are?' he suggested, having found Lydia subdued most of the afternoon, seeming to watch them all rather than taking an active part in the conversation, such as it was.

Although Scott's obvious excitement at the approach of bedtime had more than made up for any awkwardness there might have been between the adults—and there had been plenty of that, the undercurrents in this family so deep Jed hadn't had time to try and work them out yet. It appeared the little boy and his grandfather had become firm friends, which wasn't surprising; David was as warm as his youngest daughter.

'I somehow doubt that.' Meg's mouth twisted sceptically at his suggestion about her mother's motives. 'It's more likely that she meant to be insulting.'

'Hey, I take exception to that,' he chided, enjoying

teasing her. 'I'm not usually considered unacceptable to a woman's parents.' Not that he had ever met any before; his relationships didn't usually run along that line.

'Not to you, to me.' Meg sighed, laying her head back down on the pillow beside his. 'Because of Scott.'

'That's rubbish,' Jed dismissed irritably. 'He's such a cute kid, no one could feel that way about him. He and your father have definitely bonded.' David Hamilton's pleasure in his grandson was undeniable, the two having spent most of the afternoon on the floor playing with Scott's toys.

'Yes.' A smile played over Meg's lips.

Jed turned to give her a considering look. 'Do you ever see his father?'

She frowned. 'Whose father?'

'Scott's, of course,' he came back impatiently, lowering his voice as the little boy moved in his sleep. 'Do you and Scott ever see his father?'

'Certainly not.' Meg sounded shocked at the idea, forcefully so.

Jed held up a defensive hand. 'Just asking, Meg. It wouldn't be so unusual.'

'In this case it would,' she assured him determinedly, moving back to look at him. 'Why do I have the feeling that this is all research to you, and we may all appear in your next book?'

He winced, brought back to earth with a resounding bump. 'I wish,' he muttered harshly.

'What does that mean?' She looked confused.

'It means I'm not even sure there's going to be a next book.' Jed got up restlessly from the bed. 'What do you think I'm doing at the cottage in the first place?' He scowled, hands thrust into his jeans pockets. 'The public, my publishers, both here and in the States, are all clamouring for the next Jerrod Cole book. A book I haven't even written yet, and don't know if I ever will,' he admitted bleakly, putting into words for the first time the doubts he had been experiencing this last year that he could write another book—and fear that he couldn't.

The Puzzle hadn't been his first book, but his seventh, the six previous books also best-sellers, but with none of the same worldwide success or the resulting pressure to produce another runaway hit as *The Puzzle* had been.

Obviously he couldn't write another book like *The Puzzle*, had to write something completely different, but at the same time it had to be something that wouldn't disappoint all those people anxiously awaiting the next Jerrod Cole novel.

Easier said than done. In his case, writer's block had become a total shutdown. So much so that he had left New York to come to England, hoping the change would ease the pressure, accepting his editor's offer of the use of his holiday cottage in middle England, and shutting himself away there for the last two months.

It hadn't helped.

Nothing helped, his growing frustration with the situation only making things worse.

But he had, he suddenly realized, forgotten that frustration for a brief time today as he'd concentrated on Meg and her family.

Meg sat up to look at him concernedly. 'But can't

you—?' She broke off, frowning, as a knock sounded on her bedroom door followed by that door opening.

'Oh!' A slightly disconcerted Sonia stood in the doorway as they both turned to look at her. 'Sorry.' She grimaced, green gaze speculative as it moved from the standing Jed to where Meg still sat on the side of the bed. 'I just wanted to have a quick word with Meg before dinner,' she drawled, recovering quickly. 'But I can come back later.' She smiled knowingly.

So similar to look at and yet so very different.

Meg possessed none of her twin's artifice or sophistication, none of that hard gloss, either, that perfection that should have made Sonia the more beautiful of the two, and yet somehow didn't. Not to Jed, anyway.

He saw the sudden awareness of that in Sonia's eyes as they narrowed speculatively on her sister, telling Jed that this preference of her younger, less confident twin had never happened to Sonia before. That slight, angry flush to Sonia's cheeks, in Jed's opinion, boded ill for Meg.

He moved to where Meg now stood, his gaze challenging Sonia's as his arm dropped lightly about Meg's slender shoulders. 'I think that would be a good idea.' He nodded. 'After all, we wouldn't want to disturb Scott, now, would we?' he added with soft determination.

Sonia's expression became blank as it shifted to the sleeping child. 'No,' she agreed evenly. 'We certainly wouldn't want to disturb Scott.'

Jed could feel Meg's tension beneath his arm, at the same time knowing that the politeness with which the two women had been treating each other all afternoon had been nothing but another façade.

What was it with the women in this family? Having had only brothers as siblings, he wasn't as familiar with this female tension as he could have been, but he had been close to his mother all his life, all her sons were, and the strain in this family was completely unknown territory to him.

Except he knew this wasn't normal, the undercurrents between the three Hamilton women such, he felt, that if any one of them ever came out and told the other two the truth the whole structure would collapse like a house of cards.

The fact that the two sisters were still staring at each other, neither one willing to back down from whatever silent challenge was being waged, only confirmed this belief.

'We'll see you later, then, Sonia.' Jed spoke lightly but firmly, determined to break this impasse.

She flicked him an unguarded angry glance, before drawing in a deep breath and forcing the tension from her shoulders, her smile coolly confident again. 'Later,' Sonia echoed coldly before turning and leaving.

Jed's arm dropped back to his side as Meg moved away from him to stand in front of the window, although he was pretty sure she saw none of the Christmas-card whiteness of the scene outside, several more inches of snow having fallen during the afternoon.

She looked so tiny standing there, that ebony dark hair falling straight and shiny almost to her waist, very slender in the red sweater and black denims. She didn't look old enough to be Scott's mother, let alone to have all the responsibility that went along with that role.

'What the hell was all that about?' His voice sounded harsh in the silence. More so than he had intended, certainly, but it seemed the more he tried to understand this family, the less he actually knew.

Meg didn't answer for several seconds, and then she drew in a deep breath, straightening her shoulders before turning to face him, the smile she attempted reaching no further than the curve of her lips. 'It isn't important,' she dismissed.

Jed felt his frustration with the situation building inside him, his hands clenching at his sides.

It was so unimportant there were tears glistening in Meg's eyes, those eyes huge green pools of emotion in the otherwise pale stillness of her face.

'Why the hell did you put yourself through this?' he rasped impatiently. 'Put Scott through it?'

It was a low blow to bring the child she so obviously adored into the conversation, and Jed couldn't really say that Scott had suffered any harm this afternoon from his grandmother and aunt's complete indifference to his presence, his grandfather attentive enough for all of them. But that wasn't the point, was it? It wasn't going to help anyone, least of all Scott, if his mother made herself ill trying to cope with what Jed viewed as an impossible situation.

And he probably wasn't helping the situation by drawing attention to what might, for all he knew, seem perfectly normal to Meg.

'Oh, to hell with this.' He threw up his hands in disgust. 'It's your dysfunctional family. I'm sure you know how to cope with them.' He turned on his heel and walked back through the connecting doorway, closing it firmly behind him.

He didn't want any of this, didn't need it, had enough problems of his own to cope with.

Meg Hamilton would just have to deal with this herself.

The sooner the weather cleared, and he could leave, the better he would like it.

CHAPTER SIX

JED was wrong.

So very wrong.

Because Meg had absolutely no idea how to cope with all the unspoken strain in her family.

Her mother and father, she had realized as the afternoon had progressed, barely spoke to each other.

They had never been a demonstrative couple, and her mother had always been the parent whose word was obeyed, but there was a distance between her parents now that Meg didn't understand, and her father no longer mildly tolerated her mother's dictates. For instance, several times during the afternoon her mother had suggested that perhaps her father should go upstairs and rest for a while, suggestions he had completely ignored, choosing instead to play with Scott and his toys.

The strain between herself and Sonia was harder to define. Although Jed seemed to have had no difficulty picking up on it.

If not that he was part of the reason for it.

Because that was what was bothering Sonia, she was sure. Meg hadn't been home or involved with anyone since Scott was born, and now, not only had she come home for Christmas, but had apparently brought Jerrod Cole with her. The fact that she wasn't and never would be involved with Jed was something, after he had announced to her family that he was a friend of hers, none of them were likely to believe. And Sonia, being Sonia, was probably wondering just how involved with him Meg was, what confidences she might have shared with him.

As if. Sonia didn't know her at all if she thought she would ever put in jeopardy all that she had striven to achieve.

She looked up sharply as another knock sounded on her bedroom door, tensing instinctively; from not feeling wanted by her family, she had suddenly become very popular. Although another frosty encounter with her mother wasn't something she particularly relished.

She smiled her relief as she opened the door and found her father standing in the hallway, a smile on his face, and a shirt and tie draped over one arm. For Jed, she guessed. Because although he might have packed an overnight bag, she very much doubted he had packed something he could change into for dinner.

'Jed's in the room next door, Daddy,' she told him after a brief glance to make sure Scott was still asleep.

A miracle considering his excitement about the arrival of Father Christmas and the amount of visitors to their bedroom in the last few minutes.

She slipped out into the hallway to join her father. 'Are you really well again, Daddy?' She looked up at him anxiously, her hand resting lightly on his arm.

'I really am,' he returned reassuringly. 'The doctors

say it was only a mild attack. A warning, if you like, to change my lifestyle to something less stressful.'

Her father was eight years older than her mother, had retired some months ago; Meg wasn't sure how much more he could change it.

'Not in that way, pumpkin,' he said gently. 'There are certain things, about this family, that I'm not happy with. Those are the things that need changing,' he added determinedly.

She hadn't been wrong about those changes she had noticed in him, then. She knew he was physically much frailer than she remembered, but emotionally he seemed much stronger, less inclined to acquiesce to her mother for the sake of a quiet life. Could she possibly be another of those things about this family that he wanted to change?

'Yes, Meg,' he gently confirmed her thoughts. 'You're my daughter. And Scott is my grandson. I intend to see a lot more of both of you in future.'

Meg would like nothing better if it meant she only had to see her father; her mother was something else entirely.

Her father squeezed her hand sympathetically. 'It will all work out, Meg. I love your mother very much, but I love my daughters too, and now our grandson, and Lydia will have to come to terms with that.'

She didn't understand what he meant, had never understood her mother's aloofness to her family, even less so now that she was a mother herself.

Her father reached up to gently touch her cheek. 'Things aren't always what they seem, little Meg. Your mother loves you very much, and Sonia, and with time, after getting to know him, she will learn to love Scott too. It's totally impossible not to,' he added fondly.

Meg thought her father was expecting rather a lot. She had felt no softening from her mother towards Scott this afternoon, although at least she seemed to have adopted the attitude 'if you can't say anything nice then don't say anything at all'!

'And now I had better deliver these.' Her father held up the shirt and tie. 'I like him, by the way,' he added teasingly.

'Jed?' She gave him a startled look, uncomfortable with her father not knowing the truth. 'Look, Daddy, this is another case of things not being what they seem. You see,' She broke off frowningly as the bedroom door opened behind her, turning to find Jed standing there. In her bedroom.

'Sorry.' He grimaced as he saw the two of them standing in the hallway together. 'It was getting late, and I was just coming to look for you, David. For those,' he added ruefully as her father held up the shirt and tie. 'Thanks.' He took them before turning to go back the way he had come.

Probably not the best time to try and convince her father that she wasn't involved with Jed at all, that they had only met by accident, literally, the evening before.

Although quite what Jed was doing coming out of her bedroom she had no idea.

'You were saying?' her father prompted.

Meg grimaced. 'Nothing of importance.' Or, in fact, believable, in the circumstances.

Her father nodded. 'I'll just go and change for dinner

myself, then. And don't worry, Meg, everything is going to work out just fine.'

She stood and watched as he strode off down the hallway, admiring his optimism, but very much afraid he was going to be proved wrong.

But once her father had disappeared she wasted no time going through her own bedroom, but went straight to the adjacent door and into the room that connected with hers.

Only to come to an abrupt halt once she was inside, the angry words dying on her lips at the sight of Jed standing beside the bed wearing nothing but a pair of faded denims. In fact, she was having trouble breathing, let alone speaking.

Jed's chest and arms were as tanned as his face, his shoulders wide and muscled, a dark dusting of hair on his chest that went down in a vee to his stomach, not an ounce of superfluous flesh on his body.

Meg couldn't speak, couldn't move as she acknowledged she should have knocked first, that of course Jed would be changing into the clothes her father had brought him.

Jed raised one dark brow at her continued silence. 'I'm pretty sure I'm not the first half-naked man you've ever seen,' he drawled mockingly.

No, of course he wasn't. It was just that his nakedness was so unexpected, so immediate. Added to which, he was gorgeous.

His dark good looks were disturbing enough when he was fully dressed, but like this…

'I'm sorry I interrupted you and your father just now.' He grimaced. 'I thought you were in your room, and then when I heard voices in the hallway…' He broke off as she only continued to stare at him, putting the shirt down on the bed to walk slowly towards her, coming to a halt standing only inches away from her. 'You're very quiet, Meg. Don't you have anything to say now that you're here?' he queried huskily.

Something like kiss me? Take me to bed. Make love to me!

Because at that moment they were the only things she could think to say, when she could have reached out and touched the hardness of his flesh.

But she wasn't going to say any of them.

Instead she shifted her gaze away from him. Probably not a good idea either, as her gaze became riveted on the bed. A double one. Easily big enough for both of them.

'Meg?'

She swallowed hard, drawing in a deep breath as she lifted her gaze to meet his, on the assumption that looking into his eyes was better than looking at the rest of him.

But she was wrong.

Jed's eyes had darkened almost to navy as he looked down at her, that gaze shifting now to the fullness of her lips.

Meg groaned low in her throat as she felt the caress of that gaze, something melting deep inside her even as she raised her face to meet the assent of Jed's mouth on hers, moving into his arms as he pulled her against his naked warmth.

They kissed passionately, ravenously, devouring, tasting, sipping as hunger took control once again.

Jed's skin felt firm and smooth to the touch, so hot,

burning, a fire matched by one deep inside Meg, her whole body seeming to have turned to liquid flames as she clung to him, his lips moving down the sensitive column of her throat now.

'How the hell—' Jed raised his head to look at her, his hands cradling each side of her face as he gazed down at her hungrily, his fingers tangled in the dark thickness of her hair '—am I supposed to go downstairs and eat dinner with your family when it's you I want to eat?' he groaned. 'Every—' he kissed her lips '—delectable—' he kissed her again '—inch—' and again '—of you.' This time he kissed her and didn't stop.

She wanted this. As much as she might try to fight it, she wanted this, wanted Jed.

The throb of his body told her he wanted her too. Now. Urgently.

He finally dragged his mouth away from hers, breathing raggedly, his cheeks slightly flushed. 'What am I going to do with you, Meg Hamilton?' he rasped harshly.

She couldn't move, enjoying the hard curves of his body against hers, the clean male smell of him, the warmth of his skin beneath her touch. 'Do with me?' she repeated dreamily.

Jed reached up to grasp her arms and put her slightly away from him. 'I'm not sure whether you've noticed or not, but I can't keep my hands off you.' He groaned self-disgustedly.

She frowned at his tone. 'I didn't ask you to.'

'No, but—' he gave an impatient shake of his head, his hands tightening on her arms '—I'm something of a nomad, Meg. Never quite know where I'm going to be from one week to the next; have homes in New York, Vancouver and Paris. Your life is fixed here, in England, with Scott and your work. Haven't you already been hurt enough, Meg?' he added gratingly.

By Scott's father, he meant. At the same time warning her that he was no more interested in permanence than Scott's father had been. His warning would be laughable, if it didn't hurt so much.

What did Jed think she was? A single mother possibly looking for a husband for herself and a father for Scott? His talk of his nomadic lifestyle certainly seemed to indicate as much.

As quickly as her desire for this man had raged it turned to anger of equal intensity. 'Really, Jed,' she scorned as she shook off his grasp on her arm, moving away from him, eyes glittering with the force of her anger. 'You flatter yourself if you think that this—' she made a flippant gesture that encompassed everything that had happened between them in the last few minutes '—meant any more to me than it did to you.' She gave a hard laugh. 'I happen to like my life exactly as it is too, have no intention of becoming involved in a permanent relationship. Ever!' she added vehemently.

'Meg—'

'But that doesn't mean,' she continued forcefully, 'that at twenty-seven I expect to remain celibate, either. What, Jed?' she derided hardly as his expression became grim. 'Don't you like having the roles reversed on you? Too bad,' she scorned. 'Because that's the way it is. The way it will always be as far as I'm concerned.' She reached the communicating door in long strides. 'Take it or leave it.' She turned back to echo the words he had used to her this morning at the cottage.

This morning at the cottage. Uncomplicated. Simple. It seemed a lifetime away.

Jed looked at her with narrowed eyes, his mouth a thin line. 'I don't believe you, Meg,' he finally said slowly.

She gave an uninterested shrug. 'Please yourself,' she mocked. 'I usually do.'

He shook his head. 'I don't believe that, either,' he bit out. 'You wouldn't be here at all if that were really the case.'

True. Very true. She had come here for her father's sake. Because he had been ill. Because she'd been sure he'd wanted to meet Scott.

But if she had known, if she had even guessed, that she would meet Jed Cole along the way, then she wouldn't have come. Not even for her father.

Because Jed had guessed right about her. She didn't get involved in casual affairs. Never had. Never would.

So what, exactly, was she doing in Jed Cole's bedroom?

Getting out of it as fast as possible. Away from him. Away from the desire that never seemed far from the surface when she was near him.

'You must believe what you please, Jed,' she told him with dismissive scorn. 'But, in future, don't just walk into my bedroom uninvited.'

'And if I'm invited?' His jaw was squared, cheekbones hard beneath his skin, blue eyes glacial.

Meg gave a humourless smile. 'Hopefully you will be able to leave some time tomorrow. I believe I can resist temptation until then.' She went back into her bedroom, closing the door firmly, but necessarily quietly, behind her.

The tears of humiliation almost blinded her as she stumbled across the room to sit on the side of her bed, burying her face in her hands as she let those tears silently fall.

For over three years now she had kept herself deliberately aloof from any man that had shown an interest in her, not because she didn't want to love and be loved, but because she had Scott, and any man who chose to come into her life would have to be prepared to take him on too, and not just as an adjunct to her, but for himself. She had seen and heard of too many incidents where this wasn't the case, a child from a previous relationship hurt or rejected in any new relationship. She wouldn't accept that for Scott.

But she had allowed Jed Cole to get under her guard these last two days, only to have him tell her that he didn't want to get involved with her, let alone Scott, on a permanent basis. Honest, perhaps, but no less hurtful for that honesty, leaving her no choice but to defend herself.

She raised her head to look at her sleeping son, once again knowing that overwhelming rush of love for him. He was an innocent, a baby, worth all the pain of rejection she had known this last three and a half years, from her family, from so-called friends, from men like Jed Cole too, who wanted no complications in their life.

Well, you handled that really well, Jed, he told himself disgustedly as he looked at the door Meg had just closed in his face. Very suave.

Very sophisticated.

He didn't think.

But it was true that he couldn't seem to keep his hands off Meg, took every opportunity to kiss her, to hold her, whenever the two of them were alone.

And it scared the hell out of him. She scared the hell out of him.

There was no doubt in his mind that he wanted her, that the feel of her lips and body drove him wild, but he also wanted to protect her, keep her safe from harm. Even from himself, it seemed.

God, he hoped she was right about him being able to leave tomorrow—he needed to get away from Meg before she drove him insane.

But keeping his distance from Meg wasn't easy to do when he was actually staying in her parents' home, something brought starkly home to him when he found himself seated next to her at dinner.

He should have expected it, of course. There were only the six of them seated at the round table, Meg's father seated on her other side, by David's design, Jed felt sure, like two sentinels on guard.

Not that Meg looked as if she needed their protection this evening.

So far in their short acquaintance Jed had only ever seen Meg in thick sweaters and fitted denims, but somewhere in that small holdall that had comprised her own and Scott's luggage she had managed to pack the ubiquitous little black dress. A little black dress that looked sensational on Meg.

Or was it that Meg made the dress look sensational?

Whatever, he had been rendered speechless when she'd strolled into the sitting-room a short time ago to join them all for a pre-dinner drink, eyes darkly lashed, a red lip-gloss making her lips look more inviting than ever.

As if Jed needed any more invitation than just looking at her.

But Meg in that dress was something else. It had a scooped neckline, revealing the swell of her creamy breasts, with short sleeves, stopping abruptly just above her knees to reveal shapely legs and slender ankles above high-heeled black shoes. The dress was made of some sort of stretchy material that emphasized high breasts, slim waist, and curvaceous thighs, her hair free and silky down her spine.

He might have come here completely unprepared for the dressing for dinner code, but Meg certainly hadn't.

He had barely been able to take his eyes off her as she'd chatted to her father and Jeremy in the sitting-room, and now he found himself sitting next to her at the dining table, the dress having ridden up her silky thighs when she sat down, a waft of some elusive perfume stirring his senses every time she moved.

He wanted to rip the dress off her and kiss every naked, perfumed inch of her.

Sad, Cole. Very sad. Like a callow youth with a crush on a teacher. Except he wanted to teach her everything he knew.

'Salt, Jed?' David Hamilton's amused voice interrupted his obsessive thoughts.

Almost as if the other man knew what preoccupied his mind. Maybe he did, Jed accepted ruefully as he took the salt to add to his soup; there was a definite glint of laughter in those green eyes so like those of his be-witching daughter.

But this dinner was all so stilted. Jed frowned as he looked around. The conversation was polite, the table set formally with crystal glasses and silver flatware, the only concession to Christmas in this room the arrange-ment of poinsettias in the centre of the table, although the other females at the table looked as elegant as Meg, Lydia also in black, Sonia in emerald green, David and Jeremy also in formal shirt and tie.

It was a stark contrast to what would be happening at home on the farm in Montana this evening, everyone crowded into the kitchen, talking and laughing, kids yelling as his mother presided over cooking the turkey with all the trimmings. His brothers and his father would have changed into clean denims and maybe a plaid shirt, the females of the family probably having done the same.

He missed them, Jed realized heavily, missed the shouting, the laughter, the teasing, even the occa-sional arguments.

'Is the venison not to your liking, Jed?'

He focused on Sonia with effort as she sat on his right, her glittering green dress a perfect match for her eyes, eyes that were openly flirting with him, he recognized.

Venison? He looked down at the plate that had been placed in front of him. When had that arrived? Had he eaten his soup? He certainly didn't remember doing so.

You're losing it, Cole, he berated himself impatiently. Totally losing it.

But venison, for goodness' sake. Who the hell had

venison for dinner on Christmas Eve? The Hamiltons, obviously.

He couldn't help wondering what would be served for lunch tomorrow—peacock, maybe. Possibly not.

'The venison is fine, thanks, Sonia,' he replied as he realized she was still waiting for an answer.

Maybe he would go home for New Year. He had come to England to get away from the calls on his time in New York, and now, ironically, he needed to get away from England, too. Fast. If his rapidly escalating response to Meg was anything to go by.

'Are you in England for long, Jed?' Jeremy was the one to engage him in conversation now.

Almost as if some of his thoughts had shown on his face. 'I'm not sure,' he heard himself reply, and then wondered why he had been so ambiguous. The best thing for him to do was to leave England and go home, back to his roots, well away from the temptation of Meg.

'How did you and Meg meet?' Sonia took up the conversation, speculation in those green eyes now. 'I thought all of Meg's time was spent either working or looking after Scott,' she added with a sideways glance at her sister.

A glance that grated on Jed. 'Not all of it, obviously,' he drawled, easily meeting Sonia's cool gaze.

Her mouth tightened. 'Obviously not. So how did you two meet?' she persisted.

Jed easily sensed Meg's tension on his other side, one of her hands clenched on the table beside her plate. He reached out and placed his own hand over that tell-tale tension. 'Mutual friends,' he answered Sonia dismissively.

'Really?' Sonia looked surprised.

'Yes, really,' he echoed hardly. 'Meg called at my friends' cottage when I happened to be visiting. We've been inseparable ever since.' It was stretching the truth a little, although the last part was definitely true; he and Meg had rarely been apart since they'd met yesterday.

'How romantic,' Sonia drawled.

'Very.' Jed deliberately raised Meg's hand to skim his lips across the knuckles, his fingers tightening about hers as she would have instinctively pulled away from the intimacy. 'Scott's a cute kid, too.'

That hardness disappeared from Sonia's gaze to be replaced by cool blankness. 'As children go, I suppose he is.'

Jed maintained his grip on Meg's fingers, liking the feel of that tiny hand in his much larger one. 'You don't like kids?'

'I don't dislike them.' Sonia shrugged bare creamy shoulders before turning to bestow a smile on her husband. 'Although I have to admit I'm rather pleased Jeremy has children from his previous marriage and so isn't interested in having any more.'

'David, would you care to pour some more wine?' Lydia Hamilton cut firmly across what she obviously considered inappropriate dinner conversation.

And maybe it was, Jed accepted frowningly as a still silent Meg finally managed to free her hand, a hand that had trembled slightly, from his. Inappropriate, but interesting.

One twin was secure in a successful career and wealthy marriage, and obviously didn't want children to interfere with that lifestyle, whereas the other twin was unmarried and obviously not wealthy at all, and could so easily have given up the baby she would have to bring up alone, but instead was prepared to make any personal sacrifice to keep him.

He knew which twin he admired more.

Damn it.

'More wine, Jed?' David prompted lightly, bottle poised over Jed's almost empty glass.

'Why not?' Jed accepted.

Although he didn't think there was enough wine in the whole house to help him fall asleep when he went to bed later tonight.

But at least he wouldn't be alone in that wakefulness; children all over the world would be sleepless tonight as they anticipated the arrival of Santa Claus.

The difference was, his sleeplessness would have nothing to do with a jolly man in a red suit, and every-thing to do with a green-eyed witch called Meg Hamilton.

He could spend the time praying for an overnight thaw.

CHAPTER SEVEN

MEG had never been so pleased to see the end of an evening as she was this one.

The whole thing had been awful, from the embarrassing scene in Jed's bedroom, through that awkward dinner, to the equally awkward conversation when they had moved back into the sitting-room, Meg studiously avoiding so much as looking at Jed after the way he had kissed her hand in front of her whole family.

And goodness knew what he had made of the evening.

Perhaps in future he would know better than to avoid his own noisy family, if he had any sense. Tonight had been awful enough to send him running back into their midst.

Had her family always been like this? She didn't think so. It was the undercurrents of the things not being said creating the tension.

But if she was lucky she would only have to spend one more day here and then she and Scott could leave. Never to return, if she had her way. There must be a way she could arrange further meetings between Scott and her father without putting them through this again. She would find a way.

Although for the moment she had another role to play—Father Christmas to her sleeping son. Which was proving a little more difficult to do than she had anticipated. Because they had decided when they'd brought everything in earlier to hide the presents in Jed's bedroom until later tonight.

They were still there.

She had left him downstairs in conversation with her father, so perhaps if she were to just sneak in and get them... It might be a little embarrassing if he returned while she was doing the sneaking, but if she was quick...

This was ridiculous.

She was a twenty-seven-year-old woman, with a responsible job and a young son; she wasn't going to sneak anywhere in her own family home.

Not after the humiliation she had suffered earlier when Jed had warned her quite bluntly not to expect love and for ever from him. Especially not because of that. She would go where she pleased, when she pleased, and if Jed didn't like it, then tough.

But before she could make a move towards the communicating door her bedroom door opened abruptly, Sonia stepping into the room and shutting the door quietly shut behind her, her face pale as she looked across the room at Meg.

'What have you told Jed?' her sister demanded without preamble. 'Oh, don't worry,' she said impatiently as Meg glanced towards the communicating door. 'I left Jed and Daddy downstairs enjoying a brandy together.'

Sonia was so stunningly beautiful, even her present paleness giving her a look of fragile loveliness.

A look Meg knew was completely deceptive, because Sonia was hard and unyielding, caring for no one else's comfort but her own.

Meg stood up, viewing her sister dispassionately. 'I haven't told Jed anything,' she assured her with quiet dignity. 'And I never will. Not to him or anyone else. That was the idea, wasn't it?' she added contemptuously.

If anything her sister paled even more. 'You think I don't care, don't you?'

'I know you don't care,' Meg cut in purposefully. 'Who better?'

Sonia shook her head, her movements restless as she began to pace the room. 'Can I help it if I'm not like you, Meg?' she finally groaned emotionally. 'Why did you never understand?'

'But I do understand, Sonia,' she said coldly, none of her inner turmoil showing on her face. She and Sonia just didn't have conversations like this, not any more. 'You have what you wanted: your successful career and marriage.' She sighed. 'Admittedly, it's unfortunate that we've all met up in this way, but I can assure you that once we all leave here I don't care if I never see you again.' In fact, she would prefer it.

Sonia stopped her pacing, her face full of unreadable emotion, tears in her eyes. 'I miss you, Meg,' she choked.

Meg drew in a sharp, painful breath at this unexpected admission. Because the truth was, she missed her twin too. Yes, they were different, they always had been, Sonia the adventurous one, Meg usually trailing along behind in whatever mischief Sonia had dreamed up for them to do next. Yes, they were different, but as children, even initially as adults, they had shared a bond.

But it was that bond that now kept them apart.

Meg shrugged. 'You made your choices, Sonia.'

'I made a choice,' her sister corrected. 'And I still don't regret making it,' she assured softly. 'Do you?' she challenged huskily.

'Never,' Meg replied unhesitantly.

'Then why—?' Sonia groaned. 'Can't we be friends again, Meg? Daddy's illness was a shock, it made me realize life is too short, Meg.' Her twin looked at her imploringly.

This wasn't at all what she had expected from the conversation Sonia had said she wanted to have with her.

'I know what I did was wrong.' Sonia sighed emotionally. 'I know I hurt people. I hurt you. But I never meant to, Meg, it just, it just happened, and, it's Christmas, Meg, surely a time for forgiveness if ever there is one?' she encouraged softly.

This was so not what she had expected. And she didn't know what to say, what to do.

She drew in a ragged breath as Sonia continued to look at her beseechingly. 'I forgave you long ago, Sonia,' she admitted quietly. 'I think it's you, and not me, who needs to forgive yourself.'

'I've tried.' Sonia closed her eyes, a single tear escaping down the paleness of her cheek. 'Sometimes I can go for days and not—and not remember what I did.' She looked at Meg. 'But I know, all the time I know, that, given those same choices, I would do exactly the same all over again.'

Meg swallowed hard. 'Maybe acceptance is a form of forgiveness.'

'I want to be your sister again, Meg. And I want, more than anything—' her gaze was unwavering '—to be Scott's aunt.'

She frowned warily. 'You've never stopped being my sister, Sonia.' She spoke huskily. 'As for Scott—you are his aunt.'

Her sister gave a shaky smile. 'So will you try, Meg?' she asked softly. 'Will you try? For my sake if not for yours.'

Meg felt confused and uncertain. There had been antagonism between her twin and herself for so long now that she wasn't sure, in the life she had made for Scott and herself, that there was room for any other relationship with Sonia than the one they already had.

'Are you happy, Sonia?' She looked closely at her sister. 'Are you happy with Jeremy?'

'Oh, yes,' Sonia replied without hesitation. 'Oh, I know that people look at us and see summer and autumn.' Her mouth twisted ruefully. 'That people think I must have married him for his money and social standing, that he married me to have a young and beautiful trophy on his arm, but they're all wrong, Meg.' She smiled. 'I love Jeremy very much. And he loves me. We have a good life together.'

Meg nodded. 'Then that's really all that matters, isn't—?' She broke off, her eyes wide with incredulity as Jed strolled in from the adjoining room, hadn't she told him to knock the next time he came in here?

He raised dark brows as he looked at the two women,

a rueful twist to his mouth. 'Ho, ho, ho.' He looked at the bag of presents he had over one shoulder.

Meg and Sonia continued to look at him for several seconds, and then at each other, and then they both began to laugh.

'Well, I guess I know what you're getting in your stocking this year, Meg,' Sonia finally sobered enough to tease.

It was an intriguing thought, but, no, somehow Meg didn't think so.

Sonia moved gracefully, a glittering green butter-fly. 'Happy Christmas, Jed.' She reached up to kiss him on the cheek.

For longer than Meg thought necessary. Oh, she knew Sonia loved to flirt, that it came as easily to her as breathing, but nevertheless Meg couldn't help the shaft of jealousy that ripped through her at this platonic kiss.

'Happy Christmas, Meg.' Sonia moved to hug and kiss her now. 'I'm really happy for you, Meg,' she murmured so that only Meg could hear her. 'I'll see you both in the morning.' And with one last tantalizing waft of her perfume she left Meg and Jed alone in the bedroom.

Not a happy occurrence for Meg after the conversation they'd had before dinner. She watched him warily as he slowly swung the sack of presents down onto the carpeted floor.

'I heard voices in here,' he explained with a grimace. 'And from your reaction earlier to Sonia's suggestion that she would come back later, I thought you might need rescuing.'

Jed Cole to the rescue.

Once again. Except this time she didn't think she had needed rescuing.

She still felt emotional from that conversation with Sonia. It had been the last thing she had expected. Although their shared laughter at Jed's attempt at being Father Christmas was more like the two of them used to be together, so maybe, just maybe, they could start to heal this breach, after all.

'Obviously I guessed wrong—' Jed took her silence for rebuke '—but you needed these presents, anyway, right?'

Yes, she needed them, no longer had to sneak into his bedroom to get them.

'Will you for goodness' sake say something, woman?' Jed burst out impatiently.

She returned his gaze steadily. 'Thank you. I can manage from here.'

'That's it?' he rasped, thrusting his hands into his jeans pockets.

'You've barely spoken a word to me all evening and now you're dismissing me like the hired help.'

She gave him a perplexed frown. 'The only hired help I ever have dealings with is Mrs Sykes, the cook here, and as Scott and I spent a very enjoyable hour down in the kitchen with her earlier, I don't accept your accusation. She's more like one of the family.'

'Which I, obviously, am not,' he snapped.

Meg gave an irritated shake of her head. 'I thought this distance between us was what you wanted?'

He scowled darker than ever. 'You're doing this on purpose, aren't you?' he accused tersely. 'To pay me back for being so bluntly honest with you earlier.'

Her cheeks flamed with colour at this reminder of earlier. 'I think you've had too much wine and brandy.'

'Well, of course I have,' he rejoined irritably. 'What else was I supposed to do when you barely acknowledged I was sitting next to you at dinner?'

'I'm not aware that I did anything.'

'You're driving me insane, is what you're doing.' He reached out to grasp her arms, shaking her slightly. 'You look wonderful in this dress.' His gaze moved over her as impatiently as he sounded. 'I don't know how I managed to keep my hands off you during dinner. I wanted to just clear the table and make love to you there.'

She gave a mischievous smile. 'I'm sure my family would have enjoyed the spectacle.'

Jed gave a self-mocking smile. 'I'm not sure I would have cared at the time.'

She didn't understand this man. One minute he was pushing her away with talk of his nomadic lifestyle, and the next he was telling her how much he wanted to make love to her. But maybe he didn't understand himself, either.

'It's late, Jed.' She gave a shake of her head. 'I'm sure that everything will look different in the morning.' Once he had sobered up a little.

His hands dropped away from her arms. 'If the snow thaws then I'm out of here tomorrow,' he told her flatly. 'How are you going to explain that to your family?'

Why was it her responsibility? He was the one who had given her family the impression they were a couple, not her.

Her mouth firmed. 'I'm sure you'll think of something to tell them by tomorrow. Now would you please go?' she urged, lowering her voice as Scott moved restlessly in his bed, not surprising after the amount of conversations he had been a sleeping witness to this evening.

Scott was a heavy sleeper, and not much disturbed him once he was asleep, but her visitors had been excessive this evening.

Besides, she needed some time to herself to be able to think. Oh, not about Jed—all the thinking in the world wouldn't give her the answers she wanted, or change the fact that he couldn't wait to get away from here.

But she needed to digest and mull over that conversation with Sonia, to decide what to do about it, if anything. Her instinct was to do nothing, knowing that allowing herself to be close to Sonia again would change everything. She had to decide whether she wanted that change before she made any decision. And she needed time and space away from people to make it.

'Yeah, I'll go,' Jed agreed heavily once Scott had settled down again. 'But you are driving me nuts, Meg,' he paused in the doorway to murmur.

'I'm sorry,' she sighed.

He nodded abruptly, Meg only starting to breathe again once he had returned to the adjoining room and closed the door behind him.

Really, her bedroom was starting to take on the appearance of a railway station with all these comings and goings.

Although, of course, this wasn't her bedroom, only one of a number of guest rooms. Because that was what she was now: a guest.

Her own childhood bedroom, the room that had remained hers until she'd gone to live in London, was on the other side of the house. It had remained the same since she was in her teens, her cups and rosettes won at gymkhanas along one wall, some of her own drawings on another, the large bookcase full of books she had read as a child and refused to part with.

No doubt they were gone now, along with everything else in that room that had proclaimed it her room.

She blinked back the sudden tears, a part of her longing for the simplicity of those carefree days, when the biggest decision she had had to make had been the colour of her riding jacket for the day.

Jed was right: the sooner the snow thawed, and she could leave, the better she would start to feel.

Jed had no idea what the time was, or indeed where he was, totally engrossed in what he was writing.

He didn't know how or why it had happened, but at one o'clock in the morning, in the midst of a family with so many emotional problems they were too complicated for him to fathom, the storyline for a book had suddenly hit him as he'd moved restlessly about his bedroom unable to sleep. Not the storyline he had been working on so half-heartedly the last six months, either, but a totally new one, complete, entire, and urgently needing to be written down.

It hadn't taken too much effort to find David Hamilton's library, sitting down at the desk there to begin writing page after page, his own inner excitement telling him that this book was going to be as good, if not better, than *The Puzzle*.

Maybe physical frustration was exactly what he had needed to make his mind fertile again.

Because he was frustrated. Wanted Meg. Wanted her more than he had ever wanted a woman in his life before.

But he wasn't going to get her, knew that as surely as there was no thaw predicted for tomorrow.

Think positive, he told himself firmly. At least he was writing again.

He looked up as the library light was suddenly switched off, throwing him into instant darkness. 'What?' The light came on again as abruptly as it had been switched off.

David's smile was apologetic as he entered the room. 'I'm terribly sorry, Jed. I didn't know there was anyone in here. I thought someone must have forgotten to switch the light off earlier.' He stood beside the desk now, wearing a Paisley dressing gown over wine-coloured pyjamas. 'I'm sorry, have I interrupted you?' He looked down interestedly at the pile of papers covered in Jed's scrawled handwriting.

Jed sat back to flex his tired shoulder muscles. 'I could probably do with a break, anyway.' He grimaced as the hall clock struck three o'clock; he had been working for two hours without stopping—amazing after months of getting nowhere.

'Brandy?' David held up the decanter before pouring a measure into two glasses. 'I'm not really supposed to drink alcohol,' he remarked somewhat shamefacedly as the two men made themselves comfortable in the fire-side armchairs. 'But if I stopped doing everything the doctors told me to life would be pretty miserable.

'Unfortunately, the insomnia seems to be something I can do little about. Although this sometimes helps.' He sipped the brandy. 'Is Meg asleep?' he asked mildly.

Jed frowned as he looked down at the rich brown liquid in the glass he cradled in both hands. 'Things aren't—they aren't always what they seem, sir,' he said slowly, his gaze direct as he looked at the older man.

David gave a smile. 'I believe I had a conversation along similar lines with Meg this evening.'

He raised dark brows. 'On the same subject?' he prompted guardedly. 'Or something else?'

The older man's smile widened. 'I don't question my girls about their private lives, Jed.'

Jed gave David a rueful glance. 'Does the same apply to the men in your girls' lives?'

'Ah, well, that's different,' the older man came back dryly, and then chuckled at Jed's uncomfortable grimace. 'I'm not about to ask you your intentions towards Meg, if that's what's bothering you,' he assured lightly. 'I'm sure Meg is mature enough to know what she's doing.'

He wished he did.

Part of him wanted to run as fast and as far away from Meg as he could, and another part of him wanted to barricade himself in a bedroom with her for a week, so they could feast off nothing but each other.

Although he didn't think he had better share that thought with her father.

'And now I think it's time I was getting back to bed.' David drank the last of his brandy before standing up. 'If my memory serves me correctly, young children are apt to wake up very early on Christmas morning.'

Something Jed was made all too aware of only a few hours later as the age-old cry of, 'Mummy, Mummy, he's been! Father Christmas has been!' resounded in the adjoining bedroom, making Jed smile as he imagined Jed's excitement at the sackful of presents.

Although he frowned a little when he saw it was only six-thirty in the morning; he had only been asleep for three hours.

It was his own fault, of course, although he couldn't feel bad about it because he had actually written the first chapter in his new book, had the outline for the rest of it too, only needed the time now to sit down and write it. Only. This last two months in England he had had nothing but time and hadn't produced a thing worth reading.

'Ooh, Mummy, look what Father Christmas has brought me.' Scott sounded awed now. 'It's just like the one I saw in the shop and put on my list to Father Christmas.'

It was no good, Jed decided, he couldn't lie here any longer and listen to Scott's excitement through the walls. He had to be a part of what was going on in the next room.

The bright red sack that had been empty on the foot of Scott's bed the night before was now on the floor beside the bed, Scott delving excitedly into the bulging contents.

Meg looked up to give Jed a welcoming smile. 'Father Christmas has been.' She smiled, looking affectionately at her ecstatic son.

'See, Jed.' Scott lifted up the one present he had already opened, obviously the cause of his earlier excitement—a bright red tractor with a trailer on the back containing several strange looking plastic pigs.

'Hey, that's great, buddy.' He grinned as he sat down on the floor to ruffle the little boy's dark curls.

He had quickly pulled on a pair of jeans and a tee shirt before coming through from his bedroom, but Meg, so recently awakened, was still wearing her night attire: a pair of shapeless cotton pyjamas that should have looked totally unfeminine and yet on Meg didn't, only succeeding in making Jed want to take her in his arms and caress every soft curve he knew was beneath.

Very appropriate for six-thirty on Christmas morning.

'Would you like me to go and get you a cup of coffee?' he offered softly as Scott started to rip into the paper on a second present.

Meg looked surprised at the offer, making Jed realize that, living on her own with Scott, this probably didn't happen too often. If at all. Because he still didn't believe her claim about having relationships without permanence—Meg Hamilton had 'commitment or nothing' stamped all over her. It was the reason she scared the hell out of him.

She shook her head now. 'Stay and enjoy this,' she invited huskily. 'There's nothing as joyful as watching a child on Christmas morning.'

She was right: there wasn't. Jed and Meg were surrounded by presents and wrapping paper as Scott, after half an hour, found and opened the main present, right at the bottom of the huge sack, rendering the little boy speechless for several seconds.

'It's a farm, Mummy,' he finally breathed disbelievingly. 'A real farm.' His little fingers, his knuckles not yet defined, touched the farm buildings, barn, fences and assorted animals, with complete awe.

Meg, Jed saw, was blinking back the tears as she looked at the wonder on her son's face, and Jed felt a certain emotional thickness in his own throat, at the same time knowing a feeling of gratitude to Meg for letting him share this with her.

Oh, he had spent lots of Christmases on the farm with his family, his brothers' children ranging in ages from five to eleven, but the fact was they were his brothers' children, and as such Gary and Ray were the ones who got to share this magic moment with their children. Jed was just a bystander, a favourite uncle who would eventually be asked to install all the batteries in the electronic toys they had received.

This was different. Meg had made it different by inviting him to share it with her.

He stood up abruptly as he realized what was happening to him. He couldn't be— Damn it, he had barely known the woman thirty-six hours.

But as he looked down at Meg's ebony head, the long hair cascading over her shoulders, her face completely bare of make-up, her body shapeless in those unbecoming pyjamas, he knew that his worst fears had been realized.

He was falling in love with Meg Hamilton.

CHAPTER EIGHT

MEG looked up at Jed as he stood beside her, frowning at the suddenly closed expression on his face. 'What's wrong?'

'I'll go and get that coffee now,' he bit out harshly, moving abruptly away and over to the door.

Meg stared after him as he left, wondering what could possibly have happened to cause his hasty departure. Perhaps it had been the talk of Scott's farm, making him feel homesick for his own family. Or, more likely, he'd had enough of domesticity for one morning. Or perhaps he really did just need his first shot of coffee for the day.

Whatever his reasons, she very much doubted Jed was going to confide them to her.

Neither was he going to be able to leave today, she discovered as she left Scott arranging his farm to wander over to the window. The deep snow covered the ground for as far as the eye could see, like a huge white blanket, beautiful in its whiteness, but totally unsuitable for travelling.

Whether Jed liked it or not, he was stuck with them all for another day.

And he obviously didn't like it. He was totally uncommunicative when Meg and Scott made their way downstairs. Just as quiet at breakfast when they all helped themselves to food from the selection of trays set out in the dining-room.

Meg didn't feel too talkative herself when Sonia came and sat down next to her.

She still wasn't sure what to do about that conversation with her sister. Oh, she didn't want the strain between them to continue, had also missed the closeness they had once had. But she knew it was a closeness they would never be able to recapture, that too much stood between them for them to do that.

'Why don't we all go for a walk after breakfast?' Sonia suggested lightly to everyone. 'It will give Scott chance to try out his sledge,' she added encouragingly as no one responded to the suggestion.

Meg had to admit she had been stunned when she and Scott had arrived downstairs and Uncle Jeremy and Aunt Sonia had asked if they could give him his gift now.

Normally the presents under the tree, their gifts to each other rather than from Father Christmas, were opened in the early evening of Christmas Day, before they had a cold buffet dinner.

But Jeremy had explained that their gift to Scott would be of more use to him now rather than later this evening.

Meg had had to agree when Scott had ripped off the paper to reveal the wooden sledge with its gleaming runners, sure Scott was going to burst with happiness as he'd looked at it.

Scott's reaction had been obvious, but she hadn't been sure how she felt about this expensive gift to her son.

An hour later she still didn't know.

'What a good idea,' their father enthused. 'You would like that, wouldn't you, Scott? There's a little hill at the back of the house that's just perfect for sledging.'

'David, I really don't think it's a good idea for you to be—'

'Lydia, I have no intention of pulling the sledge myself,' Meg's father cut lightly across her mother's protest. 'Jeremy obviously can't do it either, with his sprained ankle, but I'm sure Jed will oblige.' He gave Jed a smile.

'Sounds good to me.' Jed nodded in agreement. 'Meg?' His gaze was unreadable as he looked across the table at her.

What a position to be in. She couldn't possibly say no, and so ruin Scott's fun, even though a part of her dearly wanted to.

For three and a half years this family had all but ignored Scott's existence, and now they were all fussing over him as if he were a treasured part of that family— it took a lot of getting used to.

She had no idea what she had expected to happen during this three-day visit, but it certainly hadn't been this.

'Yes, of course we can go sledging,' she confirmed quickly as she realized Jed was still waiting for an answer, receiving a whoop of joy and a hug from her son before he hastily began to eat his breakfast, anxious to get outside and begin.

'Are you really okay with this?' Jed caught up with her as she went upstairs to get her own and Scott's outdoor clothing.

She looked at him sharply as he fell into step beside her, obviously going upstairs for his own coat. 'Yes, of course I am. Why shouldn't I be?'

'I have absolutely no idea.' He sighed. 'I just thought I noticed a slight reluctance on your part earlier. But as far as I'm concerned this is the first normal thing this family has done since we arrived here.'

And he didn't even want to be here, she reminded herself, was only here at all because he had tried to help her and Scott.

'What would your own family be doing now?' she questioned huskily.

He shrugged. 'Sleeping, I guess. There's several hours time difference, Meg,' he added teasingly.

'I totally forgot that.' She gave a slight smile. 'Maybe you would like to call them all later? To wish them all a Happy Christmas? I'm sure my parents would be only too happy for you to use the telephone here.'

'Thanks.' He nodded. 'I'll think about it.'

She had no idea why there was this awkwardness between them now, their conversation so stilted; they had seemed perfectly okay together earlier when they had watched Scott open his presents. Before Jed had left so abruptly on the pretext of getting her coffee.

Because he never had come back with the coffee, her father bringing her a cup half an hour later when he'd come to see how Scott was doing with his presents, lingering to play with his grandson while Meg took a shower.

Not that Meg ever intended mentioning that forgotten cup of coffee; this Jed was nowhere near as approachable as the previous one.

How odd that the relationship with her family, certainly her father and Sonia, had become less strained, and now she and Jed had a distance between them that seemed insurmountable.

She grimaced. 'I'm afraid I don't have a gift to give you later today.'

'That's okay. I don't have one for you, either,' Jed responded lightly as they walked down the hallway to their bedrooms. 'How could we have?' he added harshly. 'We didn't even know each other until two days ago.'

Meg stopped, her hand on her bedroom door, looking up at him uncertainly. 'Jed, if I've done something to offend you today—'

'Why should today be any different?' he cut in dryly. 'We've been offending each other, one way or another, since the moment we met.'

She gave a pained frown. That wasn't quite true. Was it?

Admittedly, they snapped and snarled at each other occasionally, but in between that snapping and snarling they usually ended up in each other's arms.

'Don't look so worried about it, Meg,' Jed advised with a rueful smile. 'It's Christmas Day, after all.'

Yes, and, Jed apart, it was a much better Christmas Day than she had envisaged when she'd left London two days ago.

Jed apart.

Three days. That was all she had known this man. And yet already she knew he would leave a huge gap in her life when he left.

She felt herself pale, her eyes widen, as a startling truth suddenly hit her.

She was falling in love with Jed Cole.

She blinked up at him dazedly, not sure how, or even why, only knowing without a doubt as she looked into the rugged handsomeness of his face that she was falling in love with him. If she wasn't already in love with him.

And that, without a doubt, had to be the most reckless thing she had ever done in her life.

She had gone to art college at great opposition from her mother, had kept Scott to even greater opposition, and now she had managed to fall in love with a man who was totally out of her reach. Totally out of any woman's permanent reach if the things he had said to her yesterday, and his bachelorhood at the age of thirty-eight, were anything to go by.

'Are you okay?' Jed frowned down concernedly, blue gaze searching the paleness of her face.

No, she certainly wasn't okay, might never be okay again, had been stupid enough to fall in love with this man.

But it was her stupidity, and she intended keeping it to herself. There would be plenty of time to feel sorry for herself once Jed had gone.

'Just too early a start to my day, I think,' she dismissed with a shake of her head. 'Sonia's right, a walk in the fresh air is exactly what we all need.'

Jed gave her a puzzled look. 'Are the two of you okay now? I noticed the two of you seemed a little friendlier towards each other at breakfast.'

She wished she could talk to someone, to him, about the reason for the estrangement between herself and

Sonia, to ask his advice about what she should do. But she had made a promise long ago, as Sonia had made one to her, and she couldn't, wouldn't, ever break that promise. Too many people could be hurt if she did.

'Things are—better,' she answered cautiously. 'Thank you for asking.'

'That's good,' he nodded approvingly.

But he made no effort to go into his own bedroom, his gaze guarded as he continued to look down at her.

'They'll be waiting for us downstairs,' Meg mentioned huskily.

'Yes.' Still he made no move to leave.

'You have a sledge to pull up a hill,' she reminded teasingly.

His mouth curved into a smile. 'Did you see the look on Scott's face when he opened his gift and saw the sledge?'

Yes, she had seen it. And worried over it. If Sonia's idea of being Scott's aunt was just to shower him with expensive presents, then this was never going to work.

'It's what it's all about, isn't it,' Jed added softly at her silence. 'Kids at Christmas.'

Yes, it was, and perhaps she was being unfair to her sister.

'Sonia wants to start being Scott's aunt.' She only realized she had spoken her thoughts out loud as she heard herself speak, biting her bottom lip as she realized what she had done.

Jed looked at her searchingly. 'Is that going to be a problem for you?'

She drew in a sharp breath, straightening her shoulders before answering him. 'No, of course not,' she said brightly, finally turning the handle on her bedroom door and opening it. 'One big happy family at last.' That didn't come out right, she realized with a wince.

Knowing Jed had picked up on it too as his frown deepened. 'Meg, what—'

'We really do need to get back downstairs, Jed.' She gave him a bright, meaningless smile before going into her bedroom and closing the door firmly behind her.

None of this had turned out as she had expected.

None of it.

There was that difference in her father, his quiet determination to do exactly as he wished. Her sister's efforts to be friendly. And nowhere, absolutely nowhere in her imaginings had she taken into account meeting Jed Cole.

And falling in love with him.

'Need any help, Lydia?' Jed offered as she trailed behind as they walked up the hill, the other three almost at the top, Meg and Scott having insisted on pulling the sledge, Sonia pushing from behind, Scott chattering excitedly. David and Jeremy had stayed at the bottom of the hill to catch the sledge when it came down.

Jed had to admit he had been surprised when he'd returned downstairs to find Lydia Hamilton had opted to join in the sledge expedition. She seemed more the type to stay in the house where it was warm and watch from a window, if at all.

'Thank you, Jed.' She took his arm gratefully, her fashionable boots not made to climb hills slippery with snow. 'David used to do this with the girls when they were small.' She made stilted conversation.

'Did he?' Not David and I, just David, Jed noted.

Lydia gave him a quick glance, as if sensing his unspoken question, cosily warm in a long coat and hat. 'I usually stayed indoors and waited to dry them out and supply them with warm drinks when they came back in.'

Her tone was almost wistful, Jed noted, as if she longed for the days when her daughters had been small and life had been less complicated.

'Still, you've made the effort today,' he encouraged lightly, wondering if perhaps he hadn't misjudged Lydia Hamilton. When that haughty mask slipped he caught glimpses of a very lonely woman who had always stood outside her family looking in, almost as if she were afraid of the emotion held within.

Or maybe he was just imagining it, he decided ruefully as they reached the top of the hill and Lydia Hamilton slipped easily back behind that mask as she engaged her eldest daughter in conversation about mutual friends of theirs in London, taking little or no notice of her grandson as he prepared for his first sledge ride.

'Ready?' Meg prompted him, Scott already seated on the sledge, Jed having elected to go down on the first run with him.

She looked wonderful.

Wearing ankle boots and jeans, a short thick jacket over her green jumper, a red woollen hat pulled low over her ears, her hair cascading free, her cheeks flushed from her exertions up the hill, green eyes sparkling with fun.

Jed was aware of an actual physical pain as he looked

at her and then at Scott, the little boy similarly attired, his eyes excited as he waited for the off.

Anyone looking at the three of them might be forgiven for mistaking them for a real family, this woman his own, the little boy too.

He, Jed Cole, who had never considered permanence with any of the women he had been involved with over the years, let alone contemplated having children of his own, assuring his mother, whenever she teased him about his single state—which was every time he went home!—that she had enough grandchildren already without his adding to their number.

He had no doubts that his mother would like Meg. Scott too. That she would just gather the two of them in and—

Get a grip, Cole, he instantly admonished himself. Meg wasn't his. Neither was Scott. And they never would be.

He might not have believed Meg when she'd claimed that any relationships she had would be transient ones, but there had been no doubting her sincerity when she'd claimed she didn't intend getting involved in a permanent relationship. Ever!

Now wouldn't that be ironic, if, after years of avoiding the marital trap, he should happen to fall in love with a woman who had no interest in marrying him?

'Jed?' Meg's voice sounded puzzled this time as she still received no response from him.

Well…no, it wouldn't be in the least funny. Falling in love wasn't something to laugh about at all.

He really would have to get a grip, take the draft of the first chapter of his book and skedaddle out of here as fast as his long legs would carry him.

But for the moment he swung those long legs over the sledge, either side of the waiting Scott. 'All set, kiddo?' He waited only long enough for the little boy's excited nod before pushing off with his feet, his arm tight about Scott's waist as they began to slide downwards.

The cold wind rushed by his ears, Scott's scream of joy echoing in his ears, the grin on his own face irrepressible, the two of them smiling like idiots when David and Jeremy brought them to a stop at the bottom of the hill.

He was enjoying himself, Jed realized an hour later. Totally enjoying himself, none of the tensions out here that he experienced inside the house, even Sonia taking a turn on the sledge, although no amount of persuasion would induce Lydia to try it.

'That was such fun.' Sonia laughed lightly as she fell into step beside him as they all trudged back to the house a couple of hours later, not quite so perfectly turned out any more, her hair flattened by her hat, her lips bare of gloss, and looking much better for it, in Jed's opinion. More like Meg.

'It was a great present,' he answered smoothly. Meg claimed that things were better between her twin and herself, but Jed still sensed a certain restraint between them.

'Totally impractical for London, of course.' Sonia ran a hand through her flattened hair. 'But I'm sure Mother and Daddy will be quite happy for Scott to leave it here and use it when he comes to visit.'

He raised dark brows. 'Then you think there will be future visits?'

Sonia's smile faded slightly. 'I hope so.' She gave

him a considering look. 'You don't like me very much, do you?' It was a statement rather than a question.

He shrugged. 'I don't know you.' Although he had a feeling there really wasn't that much to know, no depth of character as Meg had.

'No, of course you don't.' She gave a husky laugh. 'Meg is by far the nicest of the two of us,' she added ruefully. 'Special is probably the word. Yes, Meg is very special.' She frowned slightly. 'She deserves to be happy.'

Jed raised both brows now. 'Are you warning me not to hurt your sister?'

Sonia returned his gaze unblinkingly. 'Do I need to?'

'Did you ever consider that maybe she'll be the one to hurt me?' He avoided answering the directness of her question.

Sonia gave a dismissive snort at his suggestion. 'Meg has never hurt anyone in her life.' She put a hand on his arm. 'And I think, Jed Cole, that you're a man who can be trusted with my sister's heart.'

He should be so lucky.

'Am I?' Once again he was noncommittal.

But before Sonia could answer him a snowball whizzed past the two of them to make contact, several feet away, with Jeremy's broad back.

'Who did that?' he demanded as he whirled round, eyes full of laughter as he bent to scoop up some snow, ready to retaliate.

'I cannot tell a lie.' Meg laughed as she and Scott pulled the sledge. 'It was Jed.'

Jed turned. 'Why, you little—' He didn't get time to finish as a snowball landed on the back of his head.

What followed was a complete free-for-all, snow-balls flying through the air at random, even Lydia joining in this time as one miscalculated snowball from Scott caught her squarely in the chest. There was no sub-stance to her return as it fell far short of its mark, but at least she tried.

'Hot chocolate all round, I think,' she announced once they were back at the house, tired and wet, but glowing.

'Sorry about that.' Meg walked over to join Jed as he stood in front of the window in the sitting-room looking out at the bleak, but beautiful, landscape. 'It was a game Sonia and I used to play when we were children: if we preceded a statement with "I cannot tell a lie", then we knew it was one,' she explained before taking a sip of her hot chocolate. 'What were the two of you talking about?' she questioned softly.

Lightly. Cautiously. As if his reply were important. And yet he couldn't for the life of him imagine why.

'This and that,' he answered noncommittally, contin-uing to stare out of the window.

He sensed Meg giving him a quick, searching glance. 'I wouldn't have thought the two of you had too much in common,' she finally remarked with the same light-ness as before.

And once again Jed sensed the tension behind the words. 'Not a lot, no,' he acknowledged dryly as he looked at her.

Meg gave him a reassuring smile. 'So what did you find to talk about?'

Yes, his instinct was definitely correct: Meg was worried about the conversation he'd had with Sonia.

But why? What on earth could she think her twin might have said to him that caused this concern?

He turned fully to face her, needing to see her face in order to gauge her response. 'You, mostly,' he murmured softly, and was rewarded by a brief flicker of alarm in her eyes before it was quickly masked by a return of that quizzical smile.

'Me?' She sounded surprised. 'What could Sonia possibly have to say to you about me?'

He wasn't enjoying this, Jed decided. He felt uncomfortable at Meg's forced lightness, an emotion totally belied by the way her hands were so tightly gripped about the mug of hot chocolate that her knuckles were showing white.

What he said next was purely instinctive, and completely unpremeditated. 'Meg, what's the secret that you and Sonia have between you that is so big, that it actually drives the two of you apart?'

He knew he had scored a direct hit in the question by the way Meg's face suddenly drained of all colour, the expression in her eyes no longer alarm but actual fear.

Fear.

But of what, damn it?

Because Jed had a feeling that if the secret were ever to be revealed it could be the key to all this family's seething undercurrents.

But he had absolutely no idea what it could be.

What could possibly be so important, of such magnitude, that it had kept Meg from her family since Scott had been born? Sister against sister for the same amount of time. What could have happened…

Jed turned to look across the room to where the little boy sat on the carpeted floor playing with his farm, his grandfather at his side, the two of them animated as they arranged all the animals in the appropriate pens and fields.

How could that innocent little boy, so small and carefree, possibly be the answer?

CHAPTER NINE

MEG saw the look Jed gave in Scott's direction, the speculation on his face as he continued to stare at her young son.

A speculation she had to divert away from Scott and back onto her. 'I think someone's been putting whisky in your hot chocolate, Jed,' she taunted. 'Or else your writer's block has finally broken and your imagination is running wild.' Oh, that had got his attention, that frown focused on her again now.

Which was exactly what she had wanted.

He gave her a considering look. 'As a matter of fact I was up half the night writing,' he admitted slowly.

'There you are, then.' She smiled teasingly. 'An overactive imagination and lack of sleep. You're probably hungry too after all that sledging this morning.' Too much, Meg, she realized with an inward wince as that look of speculation returned to Jed's shrewd gaze.

She literally held her breath as she waited for his reply, not wanting to have this conversation. Not now. Not here. Not ever, if she could possibly avoid it.

And it seemed, as Jed's features finally relaxed into a smile, that this time she was going to escape unscathed.

'I've been wondering about that,' he drawled. 'After the venison for dinner last night, what are we actually having for Christmas lunch?'

Meg laughed at his expression, the tension slowly starting to ease out of her at this change of subject. 'Turkey, of course,' she reassured teasingly. 'It's traditional, after all.'

'Oh, of course, and this family is big on tradition,' he said dryly.

'Some of the time we are.' She nodded.

'And does everyone fall asleep this afternoon, full of Christmas cheer?'

'We're usually full of white wine, actually,' she drawled. 'But yes, it's tra—'

'Traditional,' Jed finished lightly, his own features relaxing into a smile as Jeremy limped over to join them.

Much to Meg's relief, the conversation focused less on her as Jeremy began talking to Jed about some of the business trips he had made to America over the years, his property developing business taking him all over the world.

Nevertheless, Meg was still rather relieved when lunch was announced, sitting between Scott and her father this time, with Jed on Scott's other side, giving him no opportunity to engage her in personal conversation again.

But two hours later, all of them stuffed with turkey and Christmas pudding as well as white wine, as everyone else began to doze in armchairs, even Scott fast asleep on his grandfather's knee, Jed having disappeared upstairs as soon as the meal was finished. Meg took the opportunity to leave them all for a while. Too restless to sleep, she went down to the kitchen instead to share a cup of coffee with Bessie Sykes, the familiar warmth of the kitchen reminding her of the times she used to do this as a child.

Maybe because of that, it seemed perfectly natural, once she left the kitchen some time later, for her to go up to what had been her old bedroom, curious as to what her mother had done with it. She wanted to see whether it had been turned into yet another guest room, or maybe just a junk-room to store unused pieces of furniture until they were needed again.

She was wrong, it was neither of those things.

It was exactly the same as she had left it the last time she had stayed here over three years ago.

Nothing had been moved, nothing had been changed, the rosettes still pinned to the wall, her drawings on another, her books still on the shelves along one wall, her canopied bed, with its antique lace drapes and cover, was made up too, as if she might sleep in it that very night.

Meg was white with shock as she stepped dazedly into the room, her hand trembling slightly as she touched the music box on her lace-covered dressing-table, lifting the lid to watch the golden unicorn as it circled in time to the music.

There was no dust in here, no spider's webs, no air of neglect, the room seeming somehow to have been waiting for her return.

She closed the lid on the music box absently, moving

to the side of the bed, the pot-pourri on the bedside table smelling of fresh roses when she touched them.

Her knees felt weak as she sat down abruptly on the side of the bed to look around her.

She didn't understand.

What did all this mean? Who kept her room like this? Not Bessie, surely; she had enough to do in the rest of the house without cleaning a room that wasn't used any more. Besides, the cook/housekeeper would never have done all this without being instructed to do so. And that instruction, surely, had to have come from Lydia.

Meg really didn't understand.

Why would her mother, so cold and remote, although not quite so much today, have bothered not only to leave Meg's room as it had always been, but to keep it so…

'Is this your bedroom?'

Meg was too bemused by her discovery to do more than turn her head slowly in Jed's direction, feeling slightly numbed even as she nodded.

He strolled into the room, much as she had a few minutes ago, pausing when he reached the display of cups and rosettes she had won so many years ago.

He turned to look at her, his expression unreadable. 'Do you still ride?'

She shook her head. 'Not for the last few years; there isn't much opportunity in London.'

He shrugged. 'Maybe you should take it up again; you were obviously good. I'm sure Scott would enjoy learning to ride.'

'Maybe,' she agreed distractedly, some of the shock starting to wear off now.

What was Jed doing up here? This bedroom was on the other side of the house from the adjoining bedrooms they had been allocated yesterday, so what was he doing here.

He turned fully, leaning back against the bookcase. 'I was just going downstairs to see if I could get a cup of coffee from Mrs Sykes,' he explained as if reading her thoughts, 'when I saw you crossing the upper gallery.'

Meg frowned. 'You followed me.'

'I followed you.' He nodded, his tone gentle. 'I thought you could maybe use some company—was I wrong?' he asked huskily.

She swallowed hard, one of her hands tightly clenched in the lace cover on her bed. 'No, you weren't wrong. I thought—I thought all this—' she looked around at the beautiful feminine room '—I thought it would all be gone.' She blinked back sudden tears. 'And instead, instead I found…' She broke off, her emotions too fragile for her to continue.

'Instead you found that it's been kept exactly as you left it, yes?'

Jed moved to sit on the side of the bed beside her.

'What does it mean, Jed?' she choked, fighting to hold back the tears, knowing she hadn't succeeded as they fell hotly down her cheeks.

He reached up to gently smooth the tears from her cheeks. 'I think what it means,' he said huskily, 'is that your mother is a very complex and emotional woman that only your father truly understands.'

Her father… That conversation she had had with him last night, when he had told her that her mother loved her. This bedroom, the way it had been kept exactly as it was, surely had to mean that was true. But then why didn't her mother show that love. Why did she hold herself so aloof.

'Your mother isn't like you, Meg,' Jed soothed at her silence. 'Her emotions, whatever they might be, are kept firmly under control.'

Sonia claimed she wasn't like her, either. And yet this last couple of days Meg had discovered an emotion in both of them that she hadn't thought either was capable of. That emotion was love. Maybe they didn't in the open, giving way that Meg did, but they did love.

As she loved Jed, she suddenly saw with startling clarity. Not could. Not would. But did.

She loved the way he looked, his sense of humour, the fun he had with Scott but at the same time gentle with him, the understanding he showed her parents, the warm way he talked of his own family. But most of all, she loved him, his forcefulness when necessary, the way he had of making problems seem trivial by making her laugh at them, his intelligence.

The way he kissed her. She groaned low in her throat as he began to do exactly that.

He felt so good, tasted so good, that at that moment nothing else seemed to matter but him.

They were hungry for each other, lips and hands seeking, receiving a response that neither of them tried to deny, Meg's body turning to liquid fire as Jed touched her, and she knew he felt the same as she caressed the hardness of his back.

'You're so beautiful, Meg,' Jed rasped as he pushed her jumper aside. 'So small, perfect, and beautiful.' He groaned before lowering his head to capture one roused nipple between his lips, his hands caressing her waist and thighs.

She was on fire, needing him, all of him, wanting him so much.

A need he felt too if the heat of his body was anything to go by, his body hard with wanting her, that hardness demanding against her as he moved to lie above her.

She could feel his desire, felt her own response, her fingers feverishly entangled in the darkness of his hair as her neck arched in pleasure at the feel of his lips and tongue against her sensitized flesh, a pleasure that was building inside her, crying out for release.

A release she knew impossible as she opened her eyes to look up and see the lace canopy of her bed.

Not here, this couldn't happen here, amongst the memories of her childhood. She couldn't.

'Not here, Meg,' Jed raggedly echoed her thoughts as he began to kiss her lightly, soothingly, her neck, her cheek, her eyes, her nose, and finally her lips, his hands cupping each side of her face as he looked down at her. 'It isn't that I don't want you—I can hardly claim that at this moment, can I?' he added self-derisively, his body hard with need of her. 'I do want you, Meg, more than I would have believed possible.' He gave a pained frown. 'But this—this room…' He looked around at the trophies of her childhood.

'I feel the same way, Jed.' She reached up to touch the heat of his cheek, her smile rueful. 'It isn't right for me either. Perhaps—perhaps we should just go back downstairs and forget this ever happened?'

Forget?

He very much doubted he would ever forget the feel and taste of this woman.

But he didn't want to just make love to her for a short time, wanted days, nights, weeks with which to know her, to learn every pleasure they could give each other.

He fell back on the bed beside her, looking up at the lace canopy overhead, not knowing what to do about this woman, not knowing what to do with Meg Hamilton.

That he wanted her was in no doubt.

That she wanted him too was undeniable.

But what else did they both want? Everything? Or nothing? He couldn't go any further with this relationship until he knew the answer to that.

And he didn't think she could, either.

'We'll go downstairs.' He nodded, turning to look at her. 'But we won't forget it, Meg.' He touched one of her flushed cheeks, her eyes still dark with arousal. 'We'll talk later, hmm, when everyone else has gone to bed?'

She avoided meeting his gaze now. 'If that's what you want,' she replied noncommittally.

Jed put a hand beneath her chin to raise her face to his. 'We will talk, Meg,' he told her firmly. 'Really talk.'

He could see the slight panic in her expression he had seen earlier when she'd questioned him about his conversation with Sonia, frowning as he again wondered at the reason for it. Scott. Scott was the answer, he felt sure, but he had no idea in what way.

Or whether Meg would trust him enough, cared for him enough, to tell him.

Although none of that concern showed as they joined in the giving of presents from beneath the tree, Scott obviously enjoying his role as Father Christmas as his grandfather gave him each gift to bring in to the receiver.

This wasn't something they did in Jed's family, usually giving all the presents on Christmas morning. But this giving of the tree presents in the evening certainly carried on the anticipation of the day.

But if Meg had moved to sit as far away from Jed as possible, avoiding meeting his gaze too whenever he chanced to look her way, which was often, then Scott was certainly enjoying himself, receiving by far the most presents, several more from his mother, a ride-on tractor and trailer from his grandparents. David's doing, Jed felt sure as he watched the little boy's excitement; Lydia probably didn't have any idea of the hopes and dreams of a three-year-old boy.

Jed had even received a couple of gifts himself, a very good bottle of red wine from Sonia and Jeremy, and a first edition from David and Lydia. Again David, Jed felt sure as he warmly thanked them both.

Meg's gifts from her family, considering the rather frosty welcome she had received yesterday, were also surprising. She received a set of expensive oils from Sonia and Jeremy, and a beautiful cashmere sweater the same colour as her eyes from her parents.

'I took your father along to the shop for colour reference,' her mother explained distantly as Meg thanked them.

But there was one more small gift to be delivered, Scott's smile shy as he moved purposefully towards his grandmother.

Jed felt his own stomach muscles clench as he saw the suddenly strained look on Meg's face, the slight movement she made with her hand, as if she would like to stop Scott, that hand dropping back to her side as she decided against it.

Jed turned quickly back to look at Lydia, willing her, whatever the gift was Scott carried, not to hurt the little boy who was her grandson.

Lydia looked confused as Scott stood in front of her holding out the gaudily covered present, obviously clumsily wrapped by his own little hands. 'For me?' she said huskily, obviously completely unprepared for this. 'But I thought you and Mummy had given me a bottle of my favourite perfume?'

It was the most Lydia had spoken at one time to Scott since his arrival, and Jed could see that Meg was blinking back the tears, but the slight movement she again made to go to her son's side, in an effort of protection, Jed felt sure, was checked by her father's hand placed on her arm this time, David giving a slight shake of his head as Meg look up at him, his gaze firmly fixed on his wife.

Jed felt his own tension deepen, moving to stand at Meg's other side, knowing what she was feeling, dreading; if Lydia said or did anything to hurt Scott...

He would strangle the woman himself if she did, Jed decided fiercely.

'We did, Granma.' Scott nodded, his smile still shy.

'But we went to the shop and bought it; I made this for you myself.' He still held out the gift.

Lydia swallowed hard as she reached out to accept the gift, her face very pale beneath her make-up.

And the breath of every other person in the room was cautiously held, Jed realized as he looked at them in turn, Sonia's scarlet-tipped nails digging into Jeremy's sweater-covered arm as she clung to him, David's arm about Meg's waist now as she leant weakly against him.

Jed turned sharply back to look at Lydia, ready to leap forward and scoop Scott up in his arms if this all went terribly wrong.

'Mummy said she thought you already had one,' Scott began to chatter as his grandmother started to upwrap the present with shaking hands. 'But I made this at kindergarten for you. Do you like it?' he prompted with the innocent excitement of the very young as the unwrapped paper revealed a star painted in gold.

A slightly misshapen star, obviously made with very small, inexperienced fingers. But to Jed's eyes it was all the more beautiful for being that.

But would Lydia, a woman who never looked less than perfect herself, from her styled hair to her elegant shoes, be able to see that?

Jed felt Meg's hand slip into his, his fingers tightening reassuringly about hers as his gaze remained on Lydia.

No one moved, no one spoke as Lydia stared down at this personal gift from her grandson, the tension slowly building in that silence.

'It's for the tree.' Scott's voice began to wobble in a little uncertainty as he received no response to his gift.

Jed looked across the top of Meg's head at David, the other man deathly pale as he continued to look at his wife, but still he remained unmoving.

Couldn't he see—why didn't David do something? Anything to stop what was about to happen.

And then Lydia looked up, her face ravished with an emotion Jed had never seen there before, her eyes brimming with unshed tears.

'It's beautiful, Scott,' she gasped brokenly. 'So, so very beautiful.' The tears were falling heavily as she slid off her chair onto the carpeted floor, taking Scott in her arms to hug him as if she would never let him go. She looked up finally, attempting to smile reassuringly at her grandson. 'Let's you and I go and put it on the tree right now,' she encouraged as she stood up, the star in one hand as she reached out the other for Scott's.

'Can we?' The excitement was back in Scott's voice as he took his grandmother's hand. 'Can we really?'

'Of course we can.' His grandmother had eyes only for him as the two of them left the sitting-room together.

Jed looked quickly at Meg. There were tears on her cheeks too as she slipped beneath her father's arm, releasing Jed's hand to hurry after the unlikely pair.

Jed crossed the room in long strides, not sure what was going to happen next, only that it was going to be something momentous. And that he had to be there, for Meg, and for Scott, when it did.

CHAPTER TEN

MEG came to an abrupt halt in the cavernous hallway to stand back as her mother and Scott approached the tree together.

Her mother's tears just now had disturbed her a little. Never, in all her twenty-seven years, had she seen her mother cry, and she wasn't sure what they meant now either, only that her mother had voluntarily touched and spoken to Scott for the first time—more than touched him; she had hugged him as if he were the most precious thing in the world!

Of course, Meg already knew that he was, she just didn't know what to make of her mother thinking so too.

She turned slightly as she felt Jed's presence beside her, his narrowed gaze intent on her mother and Scott as they attempted to put the star as high up the tree as Scott held in Lydia's arms could reach.

'Do you think I should go and—?'

'No,' Jed breathed softly, turning briefly to give her a reassuring smile. 'The two of them seem to be doing just fine on their own.'

They were, yes, her mother, with Scott still in her

arms, standing back now to enjoy their handiwork, both their faces raised in wonder.

The star was no less misshapen than it had been when Scott had brought it home and insisted on wrapping it several days ago, and the glitter was no more evenly spread on its tips, and yet at that moment it was the most beautiful decoration on the tree.

'It's beautiful, Scott,' his grandmother told him chokingly. 'Absolutely perfect. Thank you so much.'

Meg felt her heart squeeze tight with emotion as Scott smiled shyly at his grandmother.

This had to be all right. It just had to be.

'What do you think, Meg? Jed?' her mother asked without turning to look at them. 'Doesn't Scott's star look absolutely wonderful on the tree?'

'Wonderful.' It was left to Jed to answer as the two of them strolled over to join them, Meg too stunned at her mother calling her Meg for the first time to be able to speak at all.

Even more so as her mother reached out and tightly clasped her hand. 'What a truly lovely son you have, Meg,' she said emotionally. 'You must be very proud of him.'

'We're all proud of him,' Meg's father echoed smilingly as he, Sonia and Jeremy came out to join them in the hallway.

'Oh, David,' her mother choked tearfully.

'My name is David too,' Scott told them excitedly as he was gathered up into his grandfather's arms. 'Sometimes, if Mummy gets cross with me, she says, "Scott David Hamilton, that was naughty!"'

The adults' laughter at this broke the tension, much

to Scott's confusion, and Meg's embarrassment. He hadn't realized he had said anything funny.

'I know, Daddy,' Sonia said laughingly. 'Let's all go and sing Christmas songs off-key around the piano, like we used to.'

Meg gave her twin a surprised look; Sonia had always hated those family singsongs at Christmas. Or, at least, she had always said that she did.

'What a wonderful idea,' their mother, another one who had always claimed she found the singing of Christmas carols tedious, agreed warmly. 'We'll start with "Jingle Bells",' she added firmly. 'I'm sure you know "Jingle Bells", don't you, Scott?' she queried as she led the way into the music room, Meg's father, Sonia and Jeremy following behind.

'What is going on?' Meg asked Jed, slightly bemused by this turn of events. And initiated by Scott giving his grandmother a gift Meg had tried to discourage him from bringing here, sure that her mother would be horrified by the imperfection that had made it all the more precious to Meg herself.

The fact that her mother seemed to feel the same way about it still stunned her.

'I have no idea,' Jed drawled, his hand light on her elbow as he turned her in the direction of the music room. 'But I should just enjoy it, if I were you.'

She did, the seven of them singing Christmas songs and carols for over an hour, her father playing the piano, the rest of them standing around it as they sang. To Meg's surprise, Jed had a rich baritone, which he put to good use.

But the embarrassment she felt every time she

looked at him was still acute; they had almost made love earlier this afternoon, and it was something she just couldn't forget.

Although Jed claimed he didn't want her to, that the two of them would talk later. Quite what that talk was going to entail—apart from the fact that any relationship between the two of them was going to be impractical and necessarily short-lived. As Jed had already pointed out, he lived wherever the fancy took him, and she was firmly rooted in London, by her work, and Scott. No, there could be no relationship between the two of them once they left here, and, as they both already knew, there could be no relationship between them here. Impasse.

But for the moment she had more surprises where her mother was concerned, Lydia insisting on coming down to the kitchen with them when it came time for Scott's tea. Much to Bessie Sykes surprise, Meg felt sure; the only time Lydia usually entered the kitchen was to discuss menus with her. Now she sat at the scarred and much-used wooden table encouraging Scott to eat his boiled egg and soldiers.

When her mother also came up to watch Scott enjoy his bath Meg felt she could contain her curiosity no longer. 'Mother, what—?'

'Not now, Meg darling,' her mother cut in softly. 'We'll get Scott to bed first, hmm, and then I think I would like to talk to all of you before dinner.'

That sounded rather ominous, but in the circumstances Meg had no choice but to acquiesce. Sitting on the side of her bed long after her mother had departed and Scott had fallen asleep, she wondered what her mother could possibly want to talk to all of them about.

But it was Christmas, after all, and perhaps a time for miracles.

'Everyone else is waiting downstairs.'

Once again Jed had come through the communicating doorway to her bedroom uninvited, but after this afternoon it would be churlish to deny him entry.

'What do you think is going on, Jed?' She gave a pained frown.

He shrugged. 'I think the thaw has probably set in in more ways than one.'

Her eyes widened before she got up and moved to the window. Jed was right—the snow was starting to melt as the temperature rose, green grass showing where the snow had already melted in patches.

Which meant Jed would be leaving soon.

But it was what she wanted, wasn't it? Jed gone, a return to her flat in London, so that she could get on with her life as she had before?

No, of course it wasn't what she wanted.

But what she wanted she knew she couldn't have, and if she had nothing else she would keep her pride.

She forced herself to smile as she turned to look at him. 'That's good news, isn't it?' she said brightly. 'You'll be able to leave in the morning now.'

'So will you,' he rasped, his eyes dark and unfathomable, his expression unreadable too.

'I'm not sure.' She shrugged. 'I may stay on another couple of days or so.' She hadn't really thought about what she was going to do after today, only intent on establishing that, just because Jed was leaving, it didn't mean she had to do so too.

Although staying on wasn't such a bad idea. Scott would love it, and her mother seemed different, since Scott had presented her with his handmade star, so perhaps she would give staying on some more thought.

It was going to be so awful when Jed got in the Range Rover and drove away.

So awful that for a moment Meg felt as if her knees were going to buckle beneath her.

He would return to the cottage, possibly even New York, and she would never see him again.

Her chest ached at the thought, her throat felt constricted, those tears that had seemed so close to the surface the last few days now blurring her vision.

'It's going to be okay, Meg,' Jed assured confidently, obviously misunderstanding the reason for those tears. 'I'm sure this talk with your mother is going to change everything.'

Perhaps that part of her life was finally going to make sense—she certainly hoped so. And until two days ago she would have been content—more than content—with that. But knowing Jed had changed all that. Now it felt, with his imminent departure, as if the bottom had dropped out of her world.

Well, it wouldn't be the first time.

And she had survived before; she would survive again.

She straightened determinedly. 'Yes, of course it is.' She nodded briskly, stepping away as Jed seemed far too close for comfort. For her control. If Jed should so much as touch her she might just break completely. And she was determined not to do that. 'If you would like to go downstairs, I'll join you all in a few minutes.'

He raised dark brows. 'You aren't going to change into that black dress again, are you?' he asked.

Her eyes widened. 'Why?' She hadn't intended to, had packed a red dress to wear this evening.

Jed shrugged. 'You look edible in that dress.' He grimaced wryly.

Meg felt her cheeks warm at the admission. 'No,' she assured him. 'I'm not wearing the black dress this evening.' The red dress, if anything, was even more figure-hugging than the black one.

'That's something, I suppose,' he drawled. 'Although I was wondering, as I'm not family—in fact, as we both know only too well, I'm actually a complete stranger—if it might not be better if I didn't join you all until later?'

His reluctance made sense, of course it did. Her family might not be aware of it, but he was really nothing but an innocent bystander—a reluctant one at that—dragged into their midst out of the snow.

But she would miss him there at her side, knew she had come to rely on his silent support over the last few days. Not a good idea, when usually she could rely on no one but herself.

Although she had a feeling, if she wanted, that might be about to change.

And she couldn't deny it would be wonderful to have the love of her family again.

Except that Jed was the man she loved.

She forced herself to give him a reassuring smile. 'Of course.' She nodded. 'I'll just explain to everyone that you're working; they're sure to understand.' It might also have the benefit of being true; she was sure Jed had been working on his book again this afternoon. 'Or perhaps you would like to go into the library and call your family?' She remembered her suggestion of earlier. 'I'm sure they would love to hear from you,' she encouraged at his continued silence.

She had been talking because of that silence, didn't understand why he had suddenly gone quiet; so far in their acquaintance she had never known Jed at a loss for words.

Perhaps it was that he would really rather leave now. The thaw was such that the main roads were sure to be clear enough to drive, and it was only ten miles or so to the cottage. Yes, maybe that was it. Jed just didn't know, with everything else that was happening, how to tell her he was leaving.

'You know, if you would like to go now, I'm sure that no one will mind,' she told him brightly, her heart squeezing painfully inside her chest just at the thought of it.

'Thanks, Meg,' he rasped harshly. 'That really makes me feel wanted.'

Wanted. She wanted him so badly she could barely breathe.

Although it seemed her remark had angered Jed. But then, nothing she seemed to say right now sounded in the least right to her, either.

'Oh, come on, Jed,' she attempted to tease. 'Admit it, you'll be glad to see the back of the Hamilton family.'

There was no answering smile on his face. 'It's certainly been different,' he allowed dryly.

'I'll bet it has.' This time her humour was genuine,

trying hard to imagine how she would have felt in his place, sitting quietly in the cottage minding his own business when someone drove into the side of that cottage, that someone turning out to be a single mother and her young son, offering, in desperation to regain that privacy, to drive them to the family home, only to become embroiled in the seething emotions of that family.

No wonder he wanted to leave.

'Time I got changed, I think,' she added firmly in an effort to hold back ready tears. 'Otherwise the family is likely to send out a search party. Too late!' She grimaced as a knock sounded softly on her bedroom door, her father entering after pausing briefly.

'We're all having champagne downstairs, if you would like to come down and join us?' he invited lightly, although the shrewd narrowing of his gaze told Meg he had picked up on the tension between Jed and herself.

'I haven't had time to change yet.'

'Oh, I shouldn't worry about that, Meg,' her father dismissed. 'It's only cold buffet for dinner, and I think we've all decided to stay exactly as we are.'

Her eyes widened at yet another change; this family always dressed for dinner.

'I believe Jed would like to stay up here and carry on with his writing.'

'Oh, no, that won't do.' Her father frowned. 'That won't do at all.' He looked steadily at the younger man.

Meg had no idea what silent words passed between the two men, only knowing that they did, Jed shrugging before announcing that he had changed his mind, that the champagne sounded inviting.

'But—'

'Leave the man alone, Meg; everyone is entitled to change their mind when there's champagne being served,' her father teased.

Except they all knew that wasn't the reason Jed had changed his mind.

And that it would only cause more embarrassment if Meg were to persist in the subject.

She gave Jed an apologetic look as they all went downstairs, receiving an encouraging smile in return, that ache in her chest only deepening at his silent support.

She hoped, for Jed's sake, if not her own, that he would be able to leave in the morning.

Jed put a hand lightly under Meg's arm and squeezed slightly as the two of them followed her father into the sitting-room where the rest of the family sat.

Meg had annoyed him earlier when she'd said he could leave now if he wanted to, but he held that annoyance in check, knowing that it wasn't his own emotions that were important just now.

But that didn't mean he wasn't still angry, or that Meg's obvious eagerness for him to leave hadn't hurt.

He followed her across the room as she chose to sit in a chair slightly away from the rest of the family, positioning himself at the side of her chair as David brought them both a glass of champagne.

'Come and sit over here, Meg,' her mother encouraged huskily, patting the space beside her on one of the two sofas in the room, Sonia and Jeremy sitting on the other one.

Jed hoped, as he and Meg moved closer into the family circle, Meg on the sofa, Jed sitting on the carpet beside her, that the fact that Lydia now called her daughter by the name she preferred had to mean something. He hoped, for Meg's and Scott's sakes, that it meant the frost between Lydia and her children was about to melt.

'First of all—' Lydia gave them all a shaky smile '—I would like to drink a toast to my wonderful husband, David, who is so much wiser and braver than me, the person responsible for us all spending this wonderful Christmas together. Thank you, David.' She held up her glass and drank, the rest of the family following her example with murmurs of 'Daddy' or 'David'. 'And to my two beautiful daughters,' Lydia continued emotionally. 'My lovely Sonia, so beautiful and accomplished. And Meg...'

Jed found himself holding his breath as he waited for what she had to say about her youngest daughter. In his eyes Meg was by far the most beautiful of Lydia's twin daughters, her inner beauty making her shine from within. But he still had no idea whether Lydia was able to see that.

'My lovely, lovely Meg.' Lydia turned to her daughter, eyes glowing with emotion. 'I'm so proud of you, Meg,' she continued huskily. 'Beautiful, warm, so filled with love, and such a wonderful mother to Scott, the sort of mother I should have been to my two daughters and was never able to be. To my two wonderful daughters.' She lifted up her glass in toast to them, the men in the room following her example.

Jed felt some of the tension ease from his shoulders, not knowing what was coming next, but more confident that it wasn't going to be anything that would hurt Meg.

Because he didn't want her hurt, happened to echo every sentiment that Lydia had just said about her. She was beautiful and warm, loved all her family in spite of their coldness towards her, and her love for her son was indisputable.

He only wished that she loved him in the same way.

But, despite what had happened between them earlier, her suggestion that he leave tonight instead of in the morning certainly didn't indicate as much.

But if Meg could be reunited with her family he would be happy for her, would have plenty of time to lick his own wounds once he was back at the cottage.

'I have one last toast I would like to make,' Lydia continued shakily, her hand reaching out to tightly grip David's as he stood supportively at her side. 'David and I had a long talk earlier, and decided to tell you all about—'

'It's all right, Lydia, I'll do it,' David said huskily. 'To our dearly loved and remembered son, James David.'

Jed felt Meg's start of surprise, a quick glance at Sonia's pale face telling him that she was as stunned by this announcement as Meg obviously was.

David and Lydia had a son? Had had a son, Jed realized as he saw the naked emotion on Lydia's face.

'James David.' Lydia sipped her champagne, not looking at any of them now but at her hand, tightly clasped within David's.

'Mummy, I don't understand,' Sonia was the one to prompt frowningly.

Lydia looked across at her daughter, her eyes swimming with unshed tears. 'We should have told you and Meg this years ago, your father wanted to, but I—I begged him not to.' She drew in a sharp breath. 'Two years before you and Meg were born your father and I had a son, a beautiful little boy, called James David, but he—he only lived for a week,' she explained emotionally. 'He was born prematurely, and, although the doctors did everything they could, he—he died.'

And that the pain of that loss was still raw within this previously emotionally aloof woman was obvious to Jed.

He couldn't even begin to imagine what it must be like to have, and then lose, a child. It must be awful, totally beyond imagination, totally beyond comprehension.

And he could see by the pain on Meg's face that she more than understood those emotions. Who better, when she had a young son of her own?

Lydia drew in another deep breath, straightening slightly. 'When I found out over a year later that I was pregnant again, with twins this time, I…I didn't think I could cope, couldn't bear it if I had to go through the pain of that loss again. And when our two daughters were born, again prematurely, weighing no more than three pounds each, my emotions simply shut down. Self-preservation, I think,' she added self-derisively.

Jed reached out and tightly clasped Meg's hand in his as he saw how badly she was shaking.

And no wonder. To learn that you had a brother, but he had died at only a week old, must be mind-numbing.

But for Lydia, he now realized, it had been so traumatic that she had been afraid to love her own daughters, too afraid that if she did she might lose them.

'To make matters worse, I was sent home, but because you were so small the two of you were kept in hospital for weeks,' Lydia continued softly. 'It was—I can't even begin to describe my feelings then. Again I came home without a baby in my arms, and although we spent every day at the hospital with you, it wasn't the same.' She shook her head, very pale.

The bonding, so necessary to this already bereft woman, simply hadn't taken place, Jed realized.

'By the time you were allowed home, I was...I wasn't very well, and your father had to do everything for you,' Lydia continued evenly, her thoughts far away now, back in the nightmare her life must have seemed then. 'But, of course, that couldn't continue, he had to return to work, and I—I was simply too ill by that time to care for you. We engaged a nanny, and I—I withdrew from you even more. It wasn't that I didn't love you, never that, I just...'

'Oh, Mummy.' Meg choked, releasing her hand from Jed's to turn to her mother, her arms going around her almost protectively. 'How awful for you. How absolutely awful.'

Sonia crossed the room swiftly, joining in the hug, the men left to look on helplessly, all of them knowing instinctively that this moment was for these three beautiful women only.

'You have to believe that I love you,' Lydia sobbed emotionally. 'That I've always loved you. I've just been too afraid to show it, too cowardly.'

'Never that,' Meg assured her firmly. 'You're the least cowardly woman I know.'

Lydia reached out and gently touched her cheek. 'You were such beautiful babies, such lovely children, but at the back of my mind was always the fear that— It's no excuse.' She shook her head with self-disgust. 'David, my darling David, decided after his heart attack that things had to change, that they would change, but even then I continued to fight him. I've been so wrong,' she choked.

'It's because of the way I've been that we aren't a closer family, that Meg, alone and so afraid when she knew she was expecting Scott, chose to keep his birth a secret for almost six months, and even after that stayed away from us all this time rather than let us help her. For that I will never forgive myself.'

Meg had chosen not to come to her parents when she had had Scott? That wasn't the impression he had got— that Meg had deliberately given him. But why had Meg stayed away. For all that Lydia had been emotionally distant, it seemed that they had offered to help her.

'If your father hadn't insisted on inviting you here for Christmas, then we would probably still be estranged.' Lydia frowned. 'All these years David has stood by and watched, loving me, loving his daughters, but not knowing how to bring us all together. It took nearly losing him a few weeks ago to bring me even partially to my senses, and even then I still held you both at a distance when you got here. But Scott, darling Scott—' her voice quivered with emotion '—although I tried to fight it, to fight loving him, was the one to bring all my barriers crashing down around my ears.' She gave a shaky smile. 'He is so beautiful, so like I imagined James would look at that age.' She broke off, too emotional to go on.

Jed felt an uncomfortable witness to this woman's heartache, and he could see by Jeremy's expression that he felt the same intrusion. This moment belonged to these three women alone.

And David, he acknowledged as Lydia turned to include him in their circle, the four of them now hugging each other so tightly there was no room for anyone or anything else.

'It's going to be so different now. I'm going to be so different. If you will let me...?' Lydia looked at them all uncertainly.

'Well, of course we'll let you,' Meg assured her with a shaky laugh. 'You're our mother, for goodness' sake.'

'Of course you are.' Sonia hugged Lydia before sitting back. 'But as this is a time for sharing secrets—'

'Sonia.' Meg cut her off sharply as she looked across at her sister.

'It's okay, Meg,' Sonia assured huskily. 'I've spoken to Jeremy, and—'

'It is not okay,' Meg rasped angrily as she stood up abruptly, her eyes deeply green in the paleness of her face.

Sonia sighed. 'Meg, I have to.'

'No, you don't.' Meg glared down at her twin, her hands tightly clenched at her sides. 'We made a pact, you and I, a pact I've kept, and I will not let you do this.'

Jed stared at the two women, as Lydia and David were now doing too, wondering what pact they could possibly be talking about. Whatever it was, Meg looked ready to do physical damage to keep it.

Sonia reached out an appealing hand. 'Meg, darling.'

'No.' Meg stepped away from that hand, breathing hard in her agitation. 'If you do this, Sonia, I swear I will never, ever forgive you.'

Sonia was as pale as her twin now, her hand dropping limply back to her side. 'I don't want to hurt you, Meg.'

'Don't you?' Meg scorned. 'Then you have a very strange way of showing it.'

'But it's all right, Meg,' Sonia insisted firmly. 'I've explained to Jeremy, and he understands.'

'I don't care whether he understands or not.' Meg was shaking with angry emotion. 'I don't understand. Do you hear me? I will never forgive you for this. Never.' She turned and almost ran from the room.

Leaving a stunned silence in her wake.

Jed was the first to move, getting abruptly to his feet, his expression grim as he quickly followed Meg from the room, having no idea what was going on, only knowing that Meg was in pain and he needed to go to her.

CHAPTER ELEVEN

MEG was quickly throwing her things into a bag when she sensed Jed had entered the bedroom, not bothering to turn and look at him, only knowing she had to get away from here. Had to call a taxi, wake Scott up, and get as far away from here as she possibly could.

Never to return.

Her hands clenched on the jumper she had been about to throw into her bag, her pain a physical thing.

To have finally made her peace with her mother, to understand her at last, had been something she had thought would never happen.

But what Sonia was about to do made any thought of a family reconciliation impossible.

'Meg, what's going on?' Jed queried softly from behind her.

What was going on? Sonia was about to shatter Meg's life into a thousand pieces, that was what was going on.

'Meg?'

'Will you just leave me alone?' She turned on him fiercely, two bright wings of angry colour in her cheeks.

He frowned darkly. 'I'm trying to understand.'

'Why?' she challenged scathingly. 'You're leaving in the morning, Jed, so why do you need to understand anything about this dysfunctional family?'

He flinched as she threw his own phrase back in his face. 'I asked you this once before: what secret do you and Sonia share that is so big it pushes the two of you apart, and you have chosen to estrange yourself from your own family because of it?'

She glared at him. 'I don't believe that is any of your business.'

'I'm making it my business,' he came back tautly.

'And I'm refusing to answer you.' she came back challengingly.

Jed became suddenly still. 'Why?' he looked at her searchingly.

'It has something to do with Scott, doesn't it?' he added with soft shrewdness.

Meg felt her face go paler even as she refused to drop her gaze from his. She had seen that speculation in his gaze earlier today as he'd looked at Scott, had managed to divert his attention then, and had no intention of satisfying his curiosity now, either.

'Did you and Sonia argue about Scott's father—is that it?' He frowned.

Meg gave him a confused look. 'What?'

Jed frowned. 'Were you involved with him and then found out that Sonia had been involved with him too—?' He broke off as Meg began to laugh. 'I'm trying to make sense of this; what the hell is so funny?' His frown deepened darkly.

Nothing. There was absolutely nothing about this

situation that was in the least funny. But Jed was so far off the mark with his speculation that it seemed funny.

Her laughter was hysteria rather than amusement, tears falling down her cheeks at the same time as she laughed.

'Let's go through to the other bedroom,' Jed muttered as Scott moved restlessly in his sleep, taking hold of Meg's arm before she had time to protest and pulling her into the adjoining bedroom, closing the door softly behind him.

Meg's tears were falling in earnest now, hot, scalding tears that burned her cheeks, her anger turning to despair.

How could Sonia do this to her? How could she just think she could tell Jeremy the truth and everything would be all right?

Because it wouldn't. There was no way Meg would give up without a fight. And it would be a fight that would rip this family apart like never before.

'Tell me, Meg,' Jed urged forcefully as he shook her slightly. 'For God's sake, tell me.'

She shook her head. 'I can't,' she choked. 'I promised that I wouldn't.'

'A promise Sonia is no longer going to keep,' he reminded softly.

Meg looked up at him, pain blinding her. 'How could she do this?' She shook her head dazedly. 'How can she even think about...about...' She sat down heavily on the bed, her face buried in her hands as the sobs racked her body.

'Meg, if you don't tell me what's going on—' Jed sat down beside her, his hands on her shoulders '—if you don't tell me then I swear I will go back downstairs and demand the truth from Sonia.'

She shook her head as she looked up at him, emotional exhaustion etched on her face.

'Meg, please.' Jed's hands fell from her shoulders. 'How can I help you if I don't know what's going on?'

'You can't help me.' She shook her head. 'No one can,' she added dully. 'And why would you even want to?' She gave a humourless smile. 'We mean nothing to you.'

'You mean something to me,' he cut in harshly. 'You and Scott both mean something to me. And if someone is trying to hurt you, then I—'

'You, what?' Meg cut in dismissively. 'You may be the rich and famous Jerrod Cole, but no amount of money can make this right.'

He stood up abruptly, looking down at her with narrowed eyes. 'That's it, I've had it,' he rasped. 'I'm going downstairs to talk to Sonia. I somehow don't think she will be as reluctant as you are to tell me the truth,' he added scathingly.

Meg watched him as he strode angrily to the door, her heart constricting as she realized she didn't want him to go, that she couldn't bear it if he left her now.

'Scott isn't my son,' she burst out emotionally, icily still as Jed slowly turned to face her. 'Scott isn't my son,' she repeated brokenly.

Jed stared across at her, unspeaking, unmoving, his expression unreadable, too.

Giving her no indication as to how he had reacted to her stark announcement.

Meg stood up restlessly, no longer looking at Jed as she began to speak again. 'Sonia had just attained her certificate to practise law, became involved with one of the junior partners in the law firm who had taken her on. A married junior partner, his wife the daughter of the senior partner,' she added dully. 'I'm sure you can guess what happened next.'

'Sonia found out she was pregnant,' Jed rasped.

'Yes,' Meg sighed. 'The two of us were sharing a flat in London at the time, sharing expenses, and when Sonia told me about the baby, that she didn't intend having it, I was horrified.' She swallowed hard. 'I persuaded her to keep the baby, told her that I would help her, that she wouldn't be alone, was convinced that once it was born she would love the baby and want to keep it.'

'But she didn't,' he murmured softly.

Meg turned away, vividly remembering the night at the hospital when Scott had been born, the way her sister had turned away from him, refusing even to hold him, Meg the one to take the newborn baby into her arms, a feeling of absolute love overwhelming her as she'd looked down at him.

But still she had been convinced that Sonia would change her mind, that it had been just a question of getting over the shock of Scott's birth, that in time her sister would grow to love her beautiful son, as Meg already had.

It hadn't happened. Scott had been given in to Meg's care when the two had been discharged from hospital, her sister resuming her job, with another law firm, and her social life, as if Scott hadn't existed. Within six months she had announced that she had met Jeremy and intended marrying him.

Leaving the question of Scott's future in the balance.

Meg hadn't carried Scott inside her, hadn't given

birth to him, but in every other way there was she had been his mother, loved him and cherished him, cared for him, played with him, laughed with him. And there had been a lot of laughter, her love for him absolute.

Sonia's announcement that she intended getting married had thrown Meg into a complete panic at the thought of losing this beautiful child.

But she needn't have worried, because Sonia had assured her she wouldn't be taking Scott with her, that Meg could keep him if she wanted to. But only if she promised never to tell anyone Scott wasn't her own.

And she never had. Had chosen to distance herself from her parents because she didn't want to lie to them, her relationship with Sonia these last three years strained at best, neither of them ever wanting anyone else to know who Scott's mother really was. Sonia because she was afraid she might lose Jeremy if he knew the truth, and Meg because she might lose Scott.

But Meg hadn't cared about any of the sacrifices she had made. Because Scott was her son. In every way that mattered, he was hers.

And she wasn't about to give him up now just because Sonia had had a belated attack of conscience.

'No, she didn't,' Meg confirmed woodenly. 'And she isn't going to take him away from me now.'

Jed's eyes narrowed. 'You think that's what she wants to do?'

Her brows rose. 'Don't you?'

'No, I don't,' he said after a brief moment of thought.

Meg gave a pained frown. 'But you heard her, she's discussed it with Jeremy.'

'She said she had told Jeremy about Scott,' Jed corrected firmly. 'Not that she wanted to take him away from you. Besides, do you really think your parents would just stand idly by while she did that to you and Scott?' he reasoned.

'But…' He was right. Jed was right, Sonia hadn't said anything about wanting Scott, only that she had told Jeremy the truth about him.

As she had just told Jed. Although it was difficult to gauge his reaction.

If he had one. After all, he would be leaving himself soon, much relieved to get away from this complicated family, she suspected.

And who could blame him?

But could he possibly be right about Sonia not wanting to take Scott away from her…?

There was only one way to find out.

Jed watched the emotions flickering across Meg's face before she rose and left the bedroom. Jed remained unmoving for several long seconds, still slightly dazed himself by what she had just told him.

What sort of woman was she, that she could take her sister's unwanted newborn son as her own?

She was the woman he loved, he acknowledged achingly. More than ever, now that he knew what she had done, the sacrifices she had made to keep Scott for her own. And the fact was, he knew that she didn't regret any of it, that if the circumstances were presented to her she would do it all over again.

She was an amazing woman.

Totally unselfish.

Totally adorable.

And he wanted to gather her up in his arms, to love, cherish and protect her, and never let her go, ever again.

Weren't they the words to the marriage ceremony?

Close enough, he realized, slightly stunned. Because that was what he wanted with Meg. Marriage. Nothing less would do.

And now was not the time to tell her that.

In fact, it couldn't have been a worse time, he acknowledged. That was him, Jed Cole, the master of bad timing.

He wanted to go downstairs right now, gather her up in his arms, and make everything right for her. But he stopped himself from doing that, knew that he didn't have the right to do that, that Meg hadn't given him that right.

That maybe she never would.

'Jed?'

He turned to see David Hamilton standing in the bedroom doorway, his handsome face lined with strain. 'Meg?' he questioned gruffly.

David gave a rueful smile. 'Jeremy and I left Meg, Sonia and their mother discussing the plans for Meg to formally adopt Scott.'

Jed raised his eyes briefly heavenwards, breathing a heavy sigh of relief as he turned back to the older man. 'Your youngest daughter is an amazing woman.'

'Isn't she?' David nodded emotionally. 'But in her own way, Sonia is just as amazing,' he said quietly. 'To know, to accept, that you can't be the mother that is needed, necessary, and to give that child up to someone who is, is very brave indeed.'

Was it? Perhaps, Jed allowed. Sonia had been twenty-three when Scott was born, abandoned in her relationship, possibly frightened of what the future might hold for her as a single mother.

Although that didn't change the fact that Meg hadn't hesitated to go through that herself for a child who wasn't actually her own.

'Yes.' David seemed to read some of his thoughts. 'But twins are a strange entity, are joined in a way that other siblings are not,' he continued frowningly. 'In some ways, Scott was always Meg's as much as he was Sonia's. Do you understand what I'm saying or does it all sound like nonsense?' He frowned at Jed.

Yes, he did understand what David was saying, and in some way that might be true. It was a little too deep for Jed to think about right now, Meg his only concern. 'Is she going to be all right, do you think?'

'Oh, yes,' the older man assured him confidently. 'Lydia and I will make sure of that. Scott has become very precious to all of us, and he will remain with his mother.'

Jed didn't doubt that the older man would keep his word, or that Lydia would ensure that he did. She surely knew better than anyone what it was like to lose a child you loved.

But that didn't stop Jed from pacing the bedroom restlessly as he waited for Meg to come back upstairs, needing to talk to her again, if only to hear from her own lips that she was going to be okay.

As it was she was the one to knock on his bedroom door, her expression somewhat shamefaced when he opened the door to her.

She grimaced. 'I believe I owe you an apology for some of the things I said to you earlier.' She sighed. 'They were unnecessary, and my only excuse—'

'Meg, I don't give a damn about any of the things you said to me earlier. And will you stop talking to me like a polite stranger?' he added impatiently, pulling her into his bedroom and firmly closing the door behind her. 'We may once have been strangers, although I don't believe that is any longer true, but we have certainly never been polite to each other,' he added ruefully.

'Oh, now I'm sure that isn't true,' Meg came back. 'We must have been polite to each other when we first met. No, perhaps not,' she added teasingly as she obviously remembered the circumstances of that first meeting.

Jed lightly cupped the sides of her face with his hands, looking down at her intently. 'Your father said… is everything all right now?' he probed huskily.

'Yes.' Her face lit up with joy. 'I'm going to adopt Scott and then he can never be taken away from me.'

Jed shook his head as he looked down at her. 'Do you know—do you have any idea—? My God, Meg.' His arms moved about her as he pulled her tightly against him. 'You are the most amazing woman I have ever met,' he told her forcefully as he buried his face in the perfumed darkness of her hair. 'I can't think of another woman I know who would have done what you did.' He groaned. 'And I want… I want…'

'Yes?' she prompted huskily as he seemed lost for words.

Because he was lost for words, had no idea how to tell this beautiful and wonderful woman, when they had only known each other three days, that he loved her, wanted to marry her, wanted her and Scott with him for all time.

CHAPTER TWELVE

NEVER in their acquaintance had Meg ever known Jed at a loss for words.

As he still seemed lost.

But she was already so happy, felt as if a great weight had been lifted from her shoulders now that the truth about Scott had finally been told and Sonia had agreed to Meg formally adopting him as her own.

It was like a dream come true for her, after years of worrying that Sonia might change her mind at any moment and decide she wanted Scott back after all. Now, that fear taken away, she felt as if she might conquer the world, or, at least, get Jed to talk to her.

'Tell me, what is it you want, Jed?' she questioned confidently.

'You,' he told her purposefully. 'I want you, Meg Hamilton.'

She wanted him too, even more than she had this afternoon, if that were possible, the truth seeming to have liberated her in more ways than one.

Okay, so he was a world-famous author, had homes all over the globe, but that didn't mean they couldn't…

Oh, goodness, he was a world-famous author with homes all over the world.

'I have no idea what you're thinking, Meg—' his arms tightened about her, his expression determined '—but I want you to know my intentions are strictly honourable.'

Strictly honourable. What did that mean?

'As in marriage,' he continued firmly. 'As in allowing me to be Scott's father. As in being my wife for the next thousand years. As in—'

'Jed, what are you talking about?' She gasped, confused, this the last thing she had expected.

'I want to marry you, Meg Hamilton. I love you, I want you, and I need you,' he said huskily. 'I realize you can't feel that way about me yet, but if you give me a chance, I'll do everything in my power to ensure that you do. I love you, Meg, and I'm not leaving here without you.' His expression was grim.

Meg stared at him. Jed loved her.

She hadn't believed that possible, had been so sure he would leave in the morning and she would never see him again. And now, now he was offering her the sun, the moon, and the stars all rolled into one, in his love for her.

Jed gave a shake of his head. 'I told myself from the beginning that I wouldn't get involved. I should have known by the mere fact that I had to tell myself that that it was exactly what I was going to do,' he muttered self-disgustedly. 'I know I was a grouch when we first met, I always am if my writing isn't going well, which it most certainly wasn't, but I'm not usually like that. Well, I am sometimes, but I'll try not to be, I really will.'

'Jed, you were perfectly entitled to feel grouchy

when we first met; I had just driven into your cottage,' Meg cut in, huskily, her happiness such now that she thought she might burst with it. Jed loved her.

'My editor's cottage,' he corrected. 'And I shouldn't have been so bad-tempered; you were a young woman and her son stranded in the snow.' He gave a self-disgusted shake of his head. 'But you frightened the hell out of me—not when you drove into the cottage,' he dismissed impatiently as she winced. 'You, you were what frightened me. I had never before desired a woman while at the same time wanting to protect her, from myself, if necessary.'

This really was all too wonderful to be true.

'And I know you've told me that you don't want a permanent relationship.'

'That was because of Scott. Any man I loved and who loved me would have to be told the truth about Scott,' she explained as he frowned. 'And it must surely be difficult enough taking on another man's child; I can't see any man wanting to take on a child who doesn't even belong to his wife.'

Jed's expression softened. 'You're looking at him. And I wouldn't be taking on Scott, I would be his father, as you are his mother. What can I say, Meg? I love the kid almost as much as I love you.'

She could see that he did, and that he had no doubts about that love.

'Jed—' she reached up to touch the hardness of his cheek '—I don't think of you as a grouch, I think of you as an amazingly kind man who has been there for me every time I needed him these last three days.'

'I don't want your gratitude, damn it.' He broke off,

giving a self-derisive grimace. 'The grouchiness may need a little working on,' he admitted ruefully.

Meg laughed huskily, her gaze steadily meeting his. 'Don't work on it too hard—I may not recognize you if you do. Because the truth is, Jed, I love you. I love you just the way you are.'

He became suddenly still, looking down at her uncertainly. 'This isn't another one of those "I cannot tell a lie" things, is it?'

'No,' she laughed again. 'We haven't known each other very long.'

'Time has nothing to do with it,' he told her firmly. 'I began to fall in love with you the moment I opened that car door in the snowstorm and saw you.'

She had probably done exactly the same thing, despite the fact that Scott had thought Jed was a bear.

Jed shook his head. 'I've been fighting against the emotion ever since, and—Meg, did you just say that you love me?' He looked slightly dazed as that realization hit him.

'I did.' She laughed softly. 'I love you, Jed,' she told him again, enjoying the freedom of being able to say those words. 'I love you, I want you, I need you,' she told him intensely. 'The thought of your leaving in the morning, of never seeing you again, has been making me totally miserable,' she admitted shakily.

'And I was furious because you couldn't seem to get rid of me fast enough.'

She looked up at him, her eyes a clear, unwavering green. 'That was my pride talking. No more misunderstandings, Jed,' she promised him.

His arms tightened around her, holding her close against him. 'Will you marry me, Meg? Will you and Scott marry me?'

'Yes,' she choked emotionally, knowing he offered her earth's version of paradise. 'Oh, yes, Jed.'

'Then I guess we did have a Christmas gift for each other, after all,' he murmured throatily, his lips only centimetres away from her own. 'Each other,' he groaned as his mouth claimed hers.

Meg had no doubts that he was the other half of her, her love, her soul mate, the person she wanted to spend the rest of her life with.

Jed held the telephone receiver to his ear, his other arm firmly around Meg as she lay curled against him in the library chair.

She was so small and beautiful, so warm and loving.

'Hi, Mom?' he prompted as his call was answered, barely able to hear his mother over the talk and laughter he could hear in the background. 'Mom, I just called to wish you all a Happy Christmas, and to tell you that I'm bringing my fiancée to meet you in a couple of days.' He held the receiver away from his ear as his mother screamed excitedly on the other end of the line.

Meg.

His fiancée. Soon to be his wife.

It couldn't happen soon enough as far as he was concerned, wanting Meg and Scott with him for all time, knowing with utter certainty that was what they would have together: for ever.

'I only have one condition to this marriage.' Jed turned to kiss Meg once he had ended the call to his family.

'We've only been engaged for an hour and you're making conditions already?' She looked up at him teasingly, eyes bright with love, her family having warmly accepted their announcement that they were to marry each other, another bottle of champagne opened as they had toasted the happy couple.

He nodded unrepentantly. 'Next Christmas we spend with my family. I don't care if we have to fly all your family over to join us, but next Christmas we spend on the farm.'

'Scott is going to love your parents' farm.' She smiled indulgently.

'So am I.' Jed grinned. 'We don't need to dress for dinner there. In fact, we may not even come down for dinner at all,' he added sensuously.

Meg laughed up at him. 'I don't care where we are, Jed, as long as we're together.'

Together.

After years of enjoying his solitude, of revelling in it, he now wanted to spend every waking hour and night with this woman, to love her, and to be loved.

The best gift of all.

HARLEQUIN *Presents*

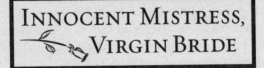

INNOCENT MISTRESS,
VIRGIN BRIDE

Wedded and bedded for the very first time

**Classic romances from your favorite
Harlequin Presents authors**

Harriet Flint turns to smolderingly sexy Roan Zandros
for a marriage of perfect convenience. But her new
Greek husband expects a wedding night to remember...
and to claim his inexperienced bride!

**Meet the next Innocent Mistress, Virgin Bride
in February 08:**

ONE NIGHT
IN HIS BED

by Christina Hollis

Book #2706

The Rich, the Ruthless and the Really Handsome

How far will they go to win their wives?

A trilogy by Lynne Graham

Prince Rashad of Bakhar, heir to a desert kingdom,
Leonidas Pallis, scion of one of Greece's leading dynasties
and Sergio Torrente, an impossibly charismatic,
self-made Italian billionaire.

Three men blessed with power, wealth and looks—
what more can they need? Wives, that's what...and
they'll use whatever means to take them!

THE DESERT SHEIKH'S
CAPTIVE WIFE
by Lynne Graham
Book #2692

Rashad, Crown Prince of Bakhar, was blackmailing Tilda over
a huge family debt—by insisting she become his concubine!
But one tiny slipup from Rashad bound them together forever....

Read Leonidas's story in

THE GREEK TYCOON'S DEFIANT BRIDE
by Lynne Graham
Book #2700
Available next month!

REQUEST YOUR FREE BOOKS!

HARLEQUIN *Presents*

PASSION
GUARANTEED
SEDUCTION

2 FREE NOVELS PLUS 2 FREE GIFTS!

YES! Please send me 2 FREE Harlequin Presents® novels and my 2 FREE gifts. After receiving them, if I don't wish to receive any more books, I can return the shipping statement marked "cancel." If I don't cancel, I will receive 6 brand-new novels every month and be billed just $3.80 per book in the U.S., or $4.47 per book in Canada, plus 25¢ shipping and handling per book and applicable taxes, if any*. That's a savings of close to 15% off the cover price! I understand that accepting the 2 free books and gifts places me under no obligation to buy anything. I can always return a shipment and cancel at any time. Even if I never buy another book from Harlequin, the two free books and gifts are mine to keep forever.

106 HDN EEXK   306 HDN EEXV

Name _____ (PLEASE PRINT) _____

Address _____ Apt. # _____

City _____ State/Prov. _____ Zip/Postal Code _____

Signature (if under 18, a parent or guardian must sign) _____

Mail to the **Harlequin Reader Service®**:

IN U.S.A.: P.O. Box 1867, Buffalo, NY 14240-1867
IN CANADA: P.O. Box 609, Fort Erie, Ontario L2A 5X3

Not valid to current Harlequin Presents subscribers.

**Want to try two free books from another line?
Call 1-800-873-8635 or visit www.morefreebooks.com.**

* Terms and prices subject to change without notice. NY residents add applicable sales tax. Canadian residents will be charged applicable provincial taxes and GST. This offer is limited to one order per household. All orders subject to approval. Credit or debit balances in a customer's account(s) may be offset by any other outstanding balance owed by or to the customer. Please allow 4 to 6 weeks for delivery.

Your Privacy: Harlequin is committed to protecting your privacy. Our Privacy Policy is available online at www.eHarlequin.com or upon request from the Reader Service. From time to time we make our lists of customers available to reputable firms who may have a product or service of interest to you. If you would prefer we not share your name and address, please check here. ☐

HP07

Men who can't be tamed...or so they think!

If you love strong, commanding men—
you'll love this brand-new miniseries.

Meet the guy who breaks the rules to get exactly
what he wants, because he is...

HARD-EDGED & HANDSOME
He's impossible to resist....

RICH & RAKISH
He's got everything and needs nobody....
Until he meets one woman...

RUTHLESS
In his pursuit of passion; in his world the winner takes all!

THE ITALIAN BILLIONAIRE'S RUTHLESS REVENGE
by Jacqueline Baird
Book #2693

Guido Barberi hasn't set eyes on his ex-wife since she left him.
He will have revenge by making her his mistress....
Can she resist his campaign of seduction?

**If you love a darkly gorgeous hero,
look out for more Ruthless books, coming soon!**

Brought to you by your favorite Harlequin Presents authors!